Chapter 1: Shadows o

Mob-Lee's one-bedroom apartment is dimly lit, cluttered with remnants of a life he's struggling to maintain. The peeling paint on the walls and a single flickering bulb above the kitchen sink reflect the state of his dwindling confidence. He sits at his worn desk, scrolling through job rejection emails on a secondhand laptop that hums noisily.

The silence is broken only by the rhythmic dripping of a leaky faucet and the low hum of the air conditioning unit struggling against the Florida humidity. Mob-Lee exhales deeply, rubbing his temples, his mind racing. He knows Tasha is coming over, and he's been replaying worst-case scenarios all day.

Suddenly, there's a sharp knock at the door—three precise raps that make his stomach tighten. He stands, adjusts his plain white t-shirt, and smooths his dark jeans as he moves toward the door, forcing a smile.

Tasha steps inside, her heels clicking sharply against the scratched wooden floor. She's dressed in a tailored beige Chanel pantsuit, her hair impeccably styled, and a subtle, intoxicating perfume fills the small space. The contrast between her polished presence and Mob-Lee's surroundings couldn't be starker.

She scans the room briefly, her expression unreadable but cold. Mob-Lee moves to embrace her, but she takes a deliberate step back, holding up a manicured hand.
"Don't," she says, her voice clipped and businesslike.

Mob-Lee hesitates, his hand dropping to his side. "What's wrong, Tasha? You barely called today."

She sighs, crossing her arms. "We need to talk."

Tasha sits on the edge of the couch, careful not to let her designer suit touch the stained fabric, while Mob-Lee remains standing.

"This isn't working, Mob-Lee," she begins, her voice firm but not unkind. "I can't keep waiting for you to figure out your life."

Mob-Lee feels the air leave his lungs. He knew this was coming but hearing it cuts deeper than he expected. "Tasha, I know I've been—"

"Stuck," she interrupts, her tone growing sharper. "You're stuck, Mob-Lee. You've been stuck since you left school. No job, no plan, no ambition. I'm out here building a future, and you're just… existing."

His hands clench into fists at his sides. "You know it's not that simple! I've been trying—"

"Trying isn't enough!" she snaps, standing now. "I've given you time. Years, Mob-Lee. And what do you have to show for it? A rundown apartment and excuses?"

Mob-Lee stares at her, struggling to form a response. His mind flashes back to the early days of their relationship when they dreamed of a future together. He never imagined it would come to this.

Tasha softens slightly, but her resolve is clear. "I'm moving on. I've already started seeing someone else. Someone who—"

"Wait," Mob-Lee interrupts, his voice cracking. "Someone else? Are you serious?"

"Yes," she says, her gaze unwavering. "He's stable. He's successful. And he's not waiting for life to happen to him."

Mob-Lee stumbles back, the weight of her words hitting him like a punch. "Tasha, please—"

"No," she says firmly, stepping toward the door. "This is goodbye, Mob-Lee. I hope you figure things out, but I can't be a part of this anymore."

Tasha leaves, the door clicking shut behind her. Mob-Lee stands frozen in place, his breath ragged. The apartment feels emptier than ever, the silence deafening. He collapses onto the couch, burying his face in his hands.

On the coffee table, her engagement ring gleams under the dim light, a cruel reminder of what he's just lost. Beside it lies a photo of them in happier times, the edges worn from years of being carried in his wallet.

The distant rumble of thunder outside mirrors the storm brewing inside him. For the first time in years, Mob-Lee feels completely and utterly defeated.

As the first drops of rain patter against the window, he clenches his jaw, a flicker of something dark and determined igniting in his chest. This isn't over. It can't be.

The sun rises over Jacksonville, casting its first rays into Mob-Lee's apartment through thin, mismatched curtains. He hasn't slept. Instead, he sits on the couch, staring blankly at a crack in the wall. His thoughts loop endlessly, replaying Tasha's departure. The engagement ring and photo still rest on the coffee table, untouched.

The silence is broken by a buzz. Mob-Lee's phone, sitting on the armrest, vibrates with a new text. At the same moment, a firm knock echoes from the front door.

Mob-Lee sits up slowly, his heart racing. Could it be Tasha? he wonders. He reaches for the phone, the screen lighting up with more incoming texts, but he hesitates. The knocking grows louder, more insistent.

"Mob-Lee Mitchell!" a deep voice calls from the other side of the door, stern and commanding.

Mob-Lee freezes, his mind racing. He peeks through the blinds cautiously. Outside, his beat-up 1989 Honda Accord looks like a relic compared to the sleek black G-Wagon parked next to it. Standing at the door is a massive man—6'7", broad-shouldered, impeccably dressed in a tailored black suit. His dreadlocks, long and manicured, rest neatly against his back.

"Logan?" Mob-Lee whispers, recognizing the figure from his past.

Mob-Lee cracks the door open, peering out at the towering man. Logan Livingston's sharp features soften into a knowing smile.

"Lil' Lee," Logan says warmly, using a nickname Mob-Lee hasn't heard in nearly a decade.

"Logan?" Mob-Lee steps back, letting the door swing open. "What are you doing here? It's been…"

"Too long," Logan interrupts, stepping inside with a measured stride. His presence fills the room, making the small apartment feel even smaller.

Mob-Lee gestures toward the couch. "Uh, sit down?"

Logan shakes his head, his smile fading. "No time for small talk. Check your phone."

Mob-Lee's phone buzzes again. He glances at it, still hoping for Tasha's name to appear. Instead, the screen is filled with texts from a single source: Aunt Camille.

Every message reads the same: "Go with Logan and welcome back, Lil Lee."

Mob-Lee's brow furrows as he reads the messages. "What the hell is this? Aunt Camille? I haven't talked to her in… since—"

Logan steps closer, his towering frame looming over Mob-Lee. "Since your family sent you away," he finishes. "I know. That's why I'm here. It's time to come back."

Mob-Lee shakes his head, taking a step back. "Come back? Back to what? I haven't heard from any of them in years. Why now? Why you?"

Logan places a firm hand on Mob-Lee's shoulder, his voice calm but unyielding. "Because you're needed. Camille sent me to bring you home. End of story."

Mob-Lee looks around the apartment, at the remnants of his life. "I need to grab a few things first."

Logan shakes his head. "Leave it. You won't need any of this anymore."

Mob-Lee hesitates, glancing around the apartment. His eyes land on the engagement ring and photo on the coffee table.

"What about—" he begins, but Logan interrupts.

"Leave it, Mob-Lee. Trust me." Logan moves to the door, holding it open.

Mob-Lee grabs his phone and wallet, then follows Logan out. As they step outside, the morning sun blinds him momentarily. The sight of the pristine G-Wagon next to his battered Honda feels surreal.

Logan walks around to the passenger side and opens the door. "Get in."

Mob-Lee hesitates, looking back at his apartment. The life he's known—however broken—is about to be left behind.

"Let's go," Logan says, his tone leaving no room for argument.

The G-Wagon's interior is immaculate, the leather seats smooth and cool against Mob-Lee's back. Logan drives with practiced ease, the engine humming as they merge onto the highway.

Mob-Lee's phone buzzes again. Another text from Aunt Camille: "Welcome home, Lil Lee. Everything is about to change."

Mob-Lee turns to Logan. "Where are we going?"

Logan glances at him briefly, a small smirk playing at the corners of his mouth. "You'll see."

As they drive, Mob-Lee feels the weight of uncertainty pressing down on him. Questions swirl in his mind, but one thought stands out above the rest: What does 'home' even mean anymore?

The G-Wagon speeds down the highway, leaving behind the crumbling remnants of Mob-Lee's old life and hurtling toward an unknown future.

Mob-Lee watches silently as Jacksonville's urban sprawl fades into the distance. The change in scenery unsettles him; the bustling streets give way to quiet open fields, stretching endlessly under the morning sun. The contrast is stark, the transition almost dreamlike.

Logan drives with calm precision, his large hands steady on the wheel. The G-Wagon's powerful engine purrs as it glides over the road.

"We've been driving forever," Mob-Lee mutters, half to himself.

Logan doesn't respond. Instead, he turns onto what looks like an unmarked dirt road, flanked by dense trees. Mob-Lee stiffens, his instincts kicking in.

"Where are we—" Mob-Lee begins, but his voice trails off as he sees them: massive iron gates rising before them, a crest with an ornate M glinting in the sunlight at their center.

Logan leans forward and presses a series of buttons on a concealed panel. The gates groan open slowly, revealing a pristine, tree-lined road stretching into the distance.

The G-Wagon moves effortlessly along the paved road, smoother than any Mob-Lee's ever seen. He leans forward, pressing his face to the window as they pass sprawling mansions, luxurious boutique shops, and manicured gardens. The area feels like a small city—a hidden world that seems far removed from anything he's ever known.

"Where are we?" Mob-Lee finally asks, his voice tinged with awe and suspicion.

Logan glances at him, a smirk tugging at his lips. "You're home, Mob-Lee… or should I say Mr. Mitchell."

Mob-Lee's eyes widen, but he says nothing.

After another turn and what feels like endless driving, the G-Wagon comes to a stop. Mob-Lee's breath catches in his throat as he takes in the sight before him: a colossal estate, larger than anything he's ever seen. The house—a mansion that resembles something out of a historical epic—dominates the landscape. Its towering columns, gleaming windows, and grand staircase make it look like a palace.

"This is your stop, Mob," Logan says, killing the engine. "Let's get you inside."

Mob-Lee steps out of the G-Wagon, his sneakers hitting the pristine cobblestone driveway. He feels out of place in his casual attire, standing before the palatial estate.

The grand double doors swing open, and a line of service staff emerges, forming an orderly row along the stairs leading up to the entrance. They stand with hands folded, their expressions poised and respectful, as though they're greeting royalty.

"Is this for me?" Mob-Lee asks under his breath, feeling a wave of discomfort.

Logan ignores the question and gestures toward the stairs. As they climb, the doors open wider, revealing two familiar figures stepping out: his twin sister, Aura-Lee, and Aunt Camille.

Aura-Lee spots Mob-Lee and gasps, her face lighting up with a mix of joy and relief. She rushes down the steps, throwing her arms around him in a tight embrace.

"Lee!" she exclaims, her voice trembling. "You're finally here!"

Mob-Lee hugs her back, momentarily lost in the familiarity of her presence. It's been years since he's seen her, but her warmth feels unchanged.

As Aura-Lee steps back, Mob-Lee's eyes shift upward to Aunt Camille, who stands at the top of the stairs, her imposing presence radiating authority. She's dressed impeccably in a dark, tailored suit, her silver hair gleaming in the sunlight.

"Lil Lee," she says, her voice calm yet commanding. "Welcome home."

Inside the grand estate, Mob-Lee feels dwarfed by the scale of the place. High ceilings, marble floors, and chandeliers create an almost surreal atmosphere.

As his eyes adjust to the grandeur, they land on two familiar faces lounging near the grand staircase. His cousins, Robert Xavier and Vance, lean casually against the railing, their expressions as mischievous as Mob-Lee remembers.

"Well, if it isn't the prodigal son," Robert says with a smirk, his sharp features betraying a hint of mockery.

Vance chuckles, crossing his arms. "Back in the fold, huh? This should be fun."

Mob-Lee's jaw tightens. Despite the years, their smug attitudes haven't changed.

Before he can respond, Aunt Camille's voice cuts through the tension. "Robert, Vance—enough. We have much to discuss, and Mob-Lee doesn't need your antics right now."

The cousins exchange glances but fall silent, their smirks lingering.

Mob-Lee looks to Aunt Camille, his mind buzzing with questions. Why now? Why here? And why did they drag him back into a family he thought had forgotten him?

Aunt Camille rests a hand on his shoulder, her gaze piercing. "Welcome to the Mitchell Estate, Mob-Lee. This is where everything changes."

Mob-Lee follows a pair of service staff through the grand estate, their measured steps echoing against the marble floors. They lead him up a sweeping staircase to the north wing.

"This is your personal wing, sir," one of them says, opening a set of ornate double doors.

Mob-Lee steps inside and is momentarily stunned. The wing feels like an entire house within itself. Seven spacious bedrooms, each with a luxurious en-suite bathroom, line the hallways. A sleek, modern kitchen gleams under recessed lighting. A cozy lounge with plush seating beckons near floor-to-ceiling windows overlooking the estate's grounds. On the third floor, a private recreation area boasts a billiards table, a state-of-the-art home theater, and even a small gym.

"Is this... real?" Mob-Lee mutters under his breath, running a hand along the polished banister of the staircase.

The staff bows slightly. "Dinner will be served shortly. Please feel free to freshen up, Mr. Mitchell."

Freshly washed but still wearing his everyday jeans and T-shirt, Mob-Lee makes his way to the dining room. The atmosphere is formal, almost stifling. The long mahogany table is set with pristine china and silverware. A chandelier casts a warm glow over the room.

As Mob-Lee takes a seat, Robert Xavier and Vance exchange smirks.

"Well, well," Robert says, leaning back in his chair. "Did you raid a thrift store on the way here, Lil Lee?"

Vance snickers. "Didn't know dinner was BYOB—bring your own broke."

Mob-Lee clenches his jaw but doesn't respond, keeping his gaze fixed on the empty plate before him.

Aura-Lee shoots them a warning glare. "Grow up, both of you."

Aunt Camille enters, her commanding presence silencing any further remarks. She sits at the head of the table and signals for dinner to be served. The staff moves swiftly, placing an elaborate spread before them.

As the meal progresses, Mob-Lee finally speaks, breaking the tension. "Alright, I've been patient. Why am I here?"

Aunt Camille sets her wine glass down carefully, her gaze steady. "To run your parents' company, of course."

Mob-Lee blinks, caught off guard. "My parents had a company? What company?"

The room falls silent, save for the faint clinking of silverware as Robert and Vance exchange amused glances.

Aura-Lee leans forward, her voice soft but firm. "We wanted you to do this, Lee. I wanted you to do this. You're the best person for it."

Mob-Lee's eyes narrow. "Why not you? You're smarter than me, and you've been here this whole time."

Aura-Lee hesitates, glancing at Aunt Camille for support. "Because I know who you are, Lee. You're the one who can bring this family back together, lead it into the future. You've always been the fighter."

Mob-Lee shakes his head, overwhelmed. "This doesn't make sense—none of it does."

Aunt Camille speaks with authority, cutting through Mob-Lee's confusion. "You'll have a few months to prepare. On September 30th—your birthdays —you and Aura-Lee will take control of the company officially. Until then, you'll learn everything you need to know."

Mob-Lee frowns. "What do I even need to do?"

"For starters," Aunt Camille continues, "you'll need to present at the Optimized Education Gala in two weeks. It's an annual event showcasing innovations in education and technology. This family always attends—and this year, you'll be the star. Prepare a proposal. Something bold."

Mob-Lee leans back, his appetite gone. The weight of it all presses on him like a lead blanket.

Meanwhile, at the other end of the table, Robert and Vance exchange hushed whispers, their mischievous smirks returning.

"If we can merge Black Sky with the Optimized Education," Robert murmurs, "we'll be able to gain control of everything."

Vance nods. "Let him play CEO. We'll make sure he crashes before he gets off the ground."

Dinner concludes, and Mob-Lee steps outside, seeking air to clear his head. The humid summer night wraps around him as he sits on the estate's grand staircase. Aura-Lee joins him, carrying two glasses of tequila.

He takes one, sipping absently. "Do you really think I can do this? Take over the company?"

Aura-Lee smiles faintly, her gaze distant as she looks out over the sprawling estate. "I don't think you can. I know you can. You're stronger than you give yourself credit for, Lee."

Mob-Lee exhales sharply, staring into the night. "I've been on my own for so long... I don't know if I even belong here."

Aura-Lee rests a hand on his shoulder. "You do. We all need you—more than you realize."

Mob-Lee nods slowly, a mix of determination and doubt flickering in his eyes. The humid air carries the faint sound of crickets, underscoring the stillness of the moment.

Above them, the estate looms like a fortress, full of secrets and challenges yet to be unraveled.

In one of the estate's dimly lit studies, Robert Xavier sits in a high-backed leather chair, drumming his fingers against the mahogany desk. Across from him, Vance lounges on a couch, swirling a glass of brandy.

"The Optimized Education Gala is our shot," Robert begins, his voice low but intense. "If we can leverage that event, Black Sky Group can position itself as the partner in revolutionizing education technology."

Vance smirks. "And what about Mob-Lee? You think he'll just let that happen?"

Robert chuckles darkly. "Mob-Lee doesn't even know what he's doing yet. He's too busy playing house. Besides, we won't go in alone."

Robert picks up his phone and scrolls through his contacts. He stops at a familiar name: Brandon Corvin, CEO of ValorTech.

"Corvin," Robert says, leaning back. "He's ruthless, hungry for power. If we can get him on board, he'll bring the kind of leverage we need to make this merger irresistible."

Vance raises an eyebrow. "And what does Corvin get out of it?"

"A piece of the pie," Robert replies with a sly grin. "And knowing Corvin, that's all he needs to hear."

Without hesitation, Robert dials the number. After a few rings, a smooth, calculated voice answers.

"Brandon Corvin speaking."

"Brandon, it's Robert Xavier. I have a business proposition you might find... lucrative."

There's a pause before Brandon responds. "I'm listening."

As Robert lays out the plan, a sharp glint of intrigue flashes in his eyes.

Mob-Lee leans against the sleek black Maybach parked outside the estate, holding his phone up for the perfect angle. The caption for his Instagram post reads:

"New life, who dis?"

With a satisfied smirk, he hits "Post." The notifications start rolling in almost immediately—likes, comments, and messages. But one notification stands out:

@TashaBeenBad liked your post.

Mob-Lee freezes, staring at the screen. His heart skips a beat. The flood of emotions—hope, regret, anger—washes over him all at once.

His thumb hovers over the message button, the urge to reach out growing stronger. *What would I even say?* he wonders.

Before he can decide, his phone buzzes with a new text message.

Aura-Lee: How's the research on Optimized Education going?

The message snaps Mob-Lee out of his haze. He stares at the text for a moment, then replies:

Mob-Lee: I think I'm going to need some help.

Almost instantly, Aura-Lee replies:

Aura-Lee: Meet me in the library in 15 minutes. We'll figure it out together.

Mob-Lee exhales, his focus shifting back to the task at hand. He puts his phone away, feeling a mix of gratitude and frustration. His sister always knew how to keep him grounded.

Mob-Lee arrives at the estate's expansive library, where Aura-Lee is already seated at a large oak table, her laptop open and several documents spread out before her.

"Glad to see you're finally taking this seriously," she says with a teasing smile.

Mob-Lee groans as he sits down. "This is way out of my league, Aura."

Aura-Lee slides a document toward him. "Not if we tackle it together. Start by understanding Optimized Education. Their mission, their projects, their partnerships. You need to know them inside and out before the gala."

Mob-Lee flips through the pages, his mind racing. "And what am I supposed to present?"

Aura-Lee leans back in her chair. "That's up to you. Think about what they need and how Mob-Lee Mitchell can provide it. Use your strengths, Lee. You've always been good at solving problems."

Mob-Lee nods, a spark of determination igniting. "Alright. Let's do this."

Meanwhile, in a sleek high-rise office in Miami, Brandon Corvin sits at his desk, his mind churning over Robert Xavier's proposal.

"Black Sky and Optimized Education," he murmurs, swirling a glass of whiskey. "If I play this right, I'll control both the education and technology sectors in Florida."

A cold smile crosses his face as he picks up his phone. "Time to make a few moves of my own."

As Mob-Lee dives into research, unaware of the schemes unfolding around him, the stage is set for a collision of ambition, betrayal, and unexpected alliances.

Chapter 2: The Game of Influence

In the dimly lit study of his wing, Mob-Lee pores over every detail about Optimized Education. The company's record is pristine—no scandals, no missteps, just consistent growth.

At the center of it all is Destiny Knight, the young CEO who seems almost too good to be true. Mob-Lee reads about her Ivy League education, sharp business acumen, and unblemished reputation.

"She's a juggernaut," he mutters. Each deal she's led has brought millions—sometimes billions—into her company's portfolio.

He leans back in his chair, staring at a photo of Destiny. Her stunning features, her poised confidence—it all begins to captivate him in ways he didn't anticipate.

Mob-Lee continues his research late into the night. Every interview, article, and financial report paints the same picture: Destiny is a woman of brilliance and precision.

But it's not just her professional prowess that intrigues him. Her natural beauty—her chocolate skin, full lips, and striking eyes—leave him mesmerized.

He scrolls through images of her at various events. "She's like a nerdy supermodel," he says, shaking his head in disbelief.

While reviewing her social media activities Mob-Lee learns that Destiny is shopping at a high-end boutique downtown from one of her live broadcasts. He decides to see her in person.

From across the street, he watches as Destiny steps out of the boutique, accompanied by her assistant. Her punctuality, her effortless grace—it all reinforces the aura of control she exudes.

"She moves like she owns the world," Mob-Lee thinks, feeling both admiration and a pang of nervousness.

After Destiny leaves, Mob-Lee enters the boutique. He approaches the tailor and casually asks about the dress Destiny purchased.

The tailor hesitates, reluctant to reveal details. But Mob-Lee's charm and persistence eventually win him over.

"It's a custom midnight blue gown with silver embroidery," the tailor says. "for a gala or something"

Mob-Lee smiles. "I'll need a suit—something that complements her dress exactly."

The tailor raises an eyebrow but agrees. "This will take a bit of time, but it'll be worth it."

Meanwhile, in one of the estate's many private lounges, Robert Xavier and Vance finalize their meeting with Brandon Corvin, the CEO of ValorTech.

They discuss the potential merger between Optimized Education and their company, Black Sky Group. They review strengths, weaknesses, and potential rebuttals for their pitch.

"Optimized Education is a massive fish," Vance says, his tone sharp and calculating. "What's stopping someone else from making a better offer?" Brandon says through the speaker.

Robert frowns. "We have no real competition. Our cousin is presenting but he's too green, I don't think he'll try to make a move."

Brandon smirks. "Either way we disrupt him before he even gets to the table."

The Robert and Vance nod in agreement, their plotting set in motion.

The next afternoon. In the opulent dining room of a Miami high-rise, Robert Xavier and Vance sit across from Brandon Corvin. The setting exudes wealth—marble floors, floor-to-ceiling windows with an ocean view, and an immaculately set lunch table.

Brandon welcomes them with a smile, his demeanor polished but calculating.

"Gentlemen," Brandon says, raising his glass of champagne. "To partnerships that bring power and prosperity."

As the three discuss final touches to their proposal for Optimized Education, Brandon subtly steers the conversation to Black Sky Group's assets, asking pointed questions about operational control and financial reserves.

Robert and Vance, eager to impress, divulge more than they should, unaware of Brandon's ulterior motives.

Later, in his private office overlooking the Miami skyline, Brandon reviews the information Robert and Vance unknowingly revealed. His smirk turns cold as he considers his true plan: a hostile takeover of Black Sky Group.

"They're desperate," Brandon mutters to himself, swirling his whiskey. "Too focused on their petty family games to see the knife at their backs."

Behind him, Tasha Sinclair steps into the room, wearing a sleek black dress.

"Everything's in place," she says. "I've already secured the necessary assets through Global Strategies."

Brandon turns to her, his eyes gleaming with satisfaction. "Good. Once we push the merger, Black Sky will be mine. And then…" His voice hardens. "They will finally pay."

Tasha's expression doesn't change, but there's a flicker of unease in her eyes.

The following day, Robert, Vance, Brandon, and Tasha board the ValorTech private jet to return to Jacksonville.

Tasha plays games on her phone engaging in light conversation. Robert and Vance, dismiss her as just another of Brandon's high-powered flings.

"You've got a good eye, Brandon," Robert jokes, nodding toward Tasha. "Looks like you're winning on and off the field."

Brandon chuckles, but his mind is elsewhere. As the jet cuts through the clouds, he silently strategizes, envisioning the steps to dismantle Black Sky once his investment secures the merger with Optimized Education.

Meanwhile, Tasha scrolls through her phone, her thumb hesitating over Mob-Lee's Instagram post, which she liked days ago. Her expression remains unreadable.

The jet lands smoothly, and the group disembarks at a private hangar.

Brandon watches as Tasha walks ahead, her confident stride matching the role she plays in his schemes. "Stay close," he murmurs to her. "We'll need your expertise soon."

Tasha nods, her thoughts a tangle of ambition, guilt, and curiosity about her former fiancé's sudden rise.

That evening, Robert and Vance return to the estate. Over dinner, they recount their Miami trip to Aunt Camille and the rest of the family, omitting key details about Brandon's deeper involvement.

Mob-Lee, sitting across the table, listens with mild interest but doesn't pry. He's focused on his research into Optimized Education and the upcoming gala.

Aura-Lee catches Mob-Lee's eye and raises a questioning brow, silently asking if he's prepared for what's to come. Mob-Lee gives a subtle nod, but his thoughts drift to the woman who's been consuming his attention: Destiny Knight.

Unbeknownst to the Mitchell family, Brandon and Tasha are already positioning their next moves, setting the stage for a storm of betrayal, ambition, and revenge…

Late afternoon Inside her stately chambers at the Federal Courthouse, Justice Camille Mitchell-Cruz sits at her polished mahogany desk, reviewing case files under the soft glow of a desk lamp. The room exudes power and authority, its shelves lined with leather-bound law books and accolades from her decades of service.

Camille presses the intercom. "Logan, step in here."

A moment later, Logan Livingston enters, his broad shoulders filling the doorway, his face calm but alert. He takes a seat across from Camille, his demeanor professional.

"Did you find out anything about Robert and Vance's trip to Miami?" Camille asks, her tone sharp.

Logan nods. "Yes, ma'am. They met with a Corvin. Brandon Corvin, CEO of ValorTech."

Camille's expression hardens. She leans back, steepling her fingers.

"They don't know, do they?" she murmurs.

Logan shakes his head. "No. Robert and Vance seem oblivious to the feud between the Corvins of Miami and the Mitchells of Jacksonville. Brandon, however, knows exactly who we are."

Camille exhales sharply, a rare sign of unease. "That family's vendetta has been festering for decades. If Brandon Corvin has made contact with Robert and Vance, he's not just looking for business. He's playing a longer, more dangerous game."

As Camille absorbs the implications of Logan's report, the desk phone rings. Camille answers, her tone authoritative.

"Justice Camille Mitchell-Cruz speaking."

A distorted voice responds. "The world will know your secrets."

Camille's grip on the phone tightens, but she maintains her composure. "Who is this?"

The line goes dead.

Camille sets the receiver down slowly. Her expression is blank, but a flicker of concern flashes in her eyes.

"The calls have started again," she says quietly.

Logan stiffens. "What do you want me to do?"

Camille meets his gaze. "Send the message. There's too much at stake now, especially with Mob-Lee back in the fold. Heighten security and surveillance around the family. No one moves without us knowing."

Logan nods and leaves the room, already making the necessary calls to implement their safety protocol.

Once Logan is gone, Camille turns her chair to face the large window overlooking the city. The courthouse stands as a symbol of law and order, but Camille knows too well that even symbols can crumble under the weight of secrets.

Her mind drifts to the Mitchell legacy, a tangled web of ambition, power, and dark truths. With Mob-Lee's return, the stakes have never been higher. The family needs him to succeed, but old enemies are circling, waiting for a moment of weakness.

Camille's fingers tremble slightly as she reaches for a photo frame on her desk. It's an old picture of her, Deacon, and Angel Mitchell. Their smiles from years past seem almost mocking now, given how much has been lost.

She sets the frame down with a resolute expression. "Not this time," she whispers to herself. "We'll win this time."

In the security headquarters of the Mitchell Estate, Logan oversees the implementation of the heightened security measures. Monitors flicker with surveillance footage of the sprawling property, and teams of personnel coordinate via headsets.

"Double the patrols," Logan orders. "I want eyes on every corner of the estate. Increase digital monitoring—phones, emails, everything. No one gets close to this family without us knowing."

A junior security officer approaches. "Sir, do you think this is related to the gala?"

Logan glances at the officer, his face stern. "I think this is related to the Mitchell name. That's reason enough to stay vigilant."

Back at the courthouse, Camille reviews the latest details on Optimized Education, Brandon Corvin, and the gala. She's connecting dots, searching for patterns, when her assistant knocks softly and enters.

"Justice Mitchell-Cruz, the Board of Governors is ready for your briefing," the assistant says.

Camille stands, smoothing her blazer. Her expression is calm and controlled, masking the storm of thoughts beneath the surface.

"Tell them I'll be there shortly."

As the assistant leaves, Camille pauses in front of a mirror on the wall, straightening her pearl necklace. Her reflection stares back at her, a reminder of the strength she must project.

"The family depends on you, Camille," she whispers to herself. Then, with one last glance, she strides out of the office, ready to face whatever comes next…

On the 18th floor of the Hyatt Regency
Brandon Corvin stands by the
floor-to-ceiling windows of his luxury suite.

Below, the Southbank of the St. John's River
glimmers with city lights reflecting off the
water. The blue hue of the Main Street Bridge
casts an ethereal glow across the landscape.

but Brandon's focus is on the phone pressed to
his ear.
"Brandon Randolph Corvin the Third," comes
the sharp voice of his father, Brandon
Randolph Corvin II, a man in his early 60s with
a commanding presence even over the phone.

"Father," Brandon replies, his tone dismissive.

"I heard what you did," his father snaps. "Threatening a federal judge? Do you even understand the risk you've just exposed us to? You're reckless!"

Brandon smirks, his eyes fixed on the shimmering water below. "They will pay for what they've done to our family. You taught me that."

"I taught you patience," his father retorts, voice rising. "You think our feud will be settled with phone calls and bold threats? Keep this up, and you'll destroy everything before we even begin.'

"Then maybe it's time for a new approach,' Brandon says coolly, ending the conversation on his terms.

He pockets the phone, his jaw tight as he stares out at the city

Brandon's thoughts are interrupted by the soft sound of Tasha Sinclair's voice behind him.

'Join me for a bath," she purrs, emerging from the bathroom wrapped in a silk robe, her curves silhouetted by the golden light behind her.
He turns, his tension melting as he takes in the sight of her. "Lead the way," he says with a sly grin,

In the expansive jacuzzi tub, steam rises, filling the mirrored bathroom with a sultry haze.

Tasha lowers herself into the water, her skin glistening as she leans back, inviting him in.

Brandon strips off his shirt, his toned physique reflecting in the mirrors that line the walls and ceiling. He slides into the water, his hands immediately seeking her out. The warmth of the water only heightens the intensity of their passion.

As their bodies intertwine, the room fills with the sound of moans and water splashing. Her nails rake down his back, his hands gripping her hips as they move together in rhythm
In the heat of the moment, Tasha cries out, "Oh, Mob!"

Brandon freezes, his movements halting for a split second.
Tasha's eyes widen, and she quickly corrects herself. "Oh, God!" she gasps, pulling him closer as if to drown out the slip.

Brandon shakes off the moment, his focus returning to her. The intensity builds again, their passion spilling over as the night continues.

The next morning, sunlight streams through the floor-to-ceiling windows of the suite. Brandon is on the phone, pacing, already deep into plans for the day before exiting.

Tasha, dressed casually, watches him leave from across the room. Her thoughts drift to the night before-to her slip, to the memories of Mob-Lee Mitchell that she couldn't shake.

She grabs her phone and scrolls through Instagram, landing on a photo Mob-Lee posted recently: another picture of sleek black Maybach. Her heart skips a beat as she realizes the luxury vehicle might not be just for show -Mob-Lee might truly be living the life he had once Talked about.

The image reignites a desire in her, a longing to reach out to him, but her phone vibrates, snapping her back to the present.

"Meet me at the hotel conference room to finalize tonight's plans," Brandon's message reads.

Tasha sighs, setting her phone down. She grabs her bag and heads out, her mind still a storm of conflicted emotions

At the boutique, Mob-Lee picks up his freshly tailored midnight blue suit with silver embroidery, a perfect match for Destiny Knight's gown.

He steps out of the shop, his confident stride drawing attention as he climbs into the black Maybach parked at the curb
Unbeknownst to him, Tasha has just arrived at the same boutique. She freezes as she spots him, her breath catching in her throat. Watching from the window, she feels her heart race as he drives away.

The sight of him-so poised, so successful- stirs a wave of emotions she thought she had buried. Memories of their time together and the man he used to be flood her mind.

"Maybe he wasn't just flexing," she murmurs to herself, recalling his Instagram post.

Inside the boutique, Tasha selects a stunning emerald gown, its elegance reflecting her desire to stand out at the gala. As the tailor wraps up her purchase, she steals another glance outside, hoping to catch a final glimpse of Mob-Lee, but he's already gone

Her phone buzzes again.

"Don't be late," Brandon's text reminds her.

She heads back to the Hyatt Regency, her thoughts a jumble of the past and present. Images of Mob-Lee flash in her mind, intertwined with memories of the passionate night she spent with Brandon.

By the time she returns to the suite, she's resolved to focus on the night ahead. But deep down, she knows her feelings for Mob-Lee are far from resolved.

As the sun begins to set over the city, the vibrant hues of orange and pink paint the sky. In the library of the Mitchell Estate, Mob-Lee meticulously reviews his presentation with his sister, Aura-Lee. The room is filled with an air of quiet concentration as slides flash across his laptop screen.

Aura-Lee sits across from him, her eyes wide with admiration. "This is incredible, Lee. Your analysis is razor-sharp. The way you've structured everything—" she pauses, smiling. "It's amazing how perfect this is without you even mentioning the company's name."

Mob-Lee looks up, his brow furrowed. "You know, that's been bothering me. Nobody's ever told me the name of this business I'm supposed to be helping pitch for."

Aura-Lee chuckles, leaning back in her chair. "That's on purpose. Aunt Cammy said it was better if you went into this blind, focused on the numbers and strategy, not the legacy. But since we're here..."

She leans in conspiratorially. "The official name is Mitchell Global Strategies Firm, but everyone just calls it Global Strategies. It's a staple in the business world. The name carries weight, but honestly? It doesn't even matter. Your presentation stands on its own."

Mob-Lee nods, absorbing the information. "Mitchell Global Strategies," he repeats, the name settling over him like a cloak of responsibility. "Well, legacy or not, I'm ready."

Meanwhile, in the east wing of the estate, Robert Xavier and Vance Cruz host an impromptu pre-gala celebration. The room buzzes with the sound of laughter, clinking glasses, and boisterous conversation as a group of wealthy friends and acquaintances revel in the lavish surroundings.

Robert, already several drinks in, raises his glass. "To tonight! By this time tomorrow, our partnership with Optimized Education will be the talk of the business world. They have no choice but to approve the merger."

Vance smirks, swirling his drink. "And with Brandon Corvin on our side, we're untouchable."

Unbeknownst to them, Brandon has no intention of remaining their ally.

The party continues, their overconfidence blinding them to the storm brewing around them.

In her suite at the Hyatt Regency, Tasha Sinclair sits at her desk, reviewing the final steps of her plan. She's worked tirelessly to position herself as the Vice President of Operations for Global Strategies, leveraging her role to quietly divert assets from Black Sky Group, to ValorTech.

A knock at the door interrupts her thoughts. Brandon steps in, impeccably dressed in a tailored suit. "Is everything ready?" he asks, his tone sharp.

Tasha nods, handing him a file. "Every detail is in place. Once the merger is announced, you'll have majority control over Black Sky. They will be none the wiser—at least not until it's too late."

Brandon smirks, taking the file. "Good. After tonight, they won't know what hit them."

Tasha watches him leave, her thoughts flickering to Mob-Lee. Despite her loyalty to Brandon, memories of her former fiancé linger, complicating her resolve.

Back in the main house, Aunt Camille and Logan Livingston finalize the security protocols for the evening. Camille's tone is firm as she instructs Logan. "The family's safety comes first. No deviations. Every vehicle in the convoy must stay within the formation."

Logan nods. "Understood. I've already briefed the security detail. We'll be monitoring everything in real time."

Camille sighs, glancing at the clock. "There's too much at stake tonight, Logan. We can't afford any missteps."

As the time nears, the Mitchell family begins to gather in the grand foyer. Dressed in their finest, they exude an air of elegance and power. Mob-Lee, in his tailored midnight blue suit with silver embroidery, stands out, his confidence evident.

The convoy of black SUVs pulls up to the estate's entrance, their sleek design reflecting the evening's fading light. One by one, the Mitchells file into the vehicles, their faces a mixture of nerves and determination.

Mob-Lee sits quietly, going over his presentation in his mind. Aura-Lee, seated beside him, gives his arm a reassuring squeeze. "You've got this."

In another SUV, Robert and Vance exchange smug glances, their overconfidence bolstered by the alcohol still coursing through their veins.

The tension is pulsing as the convoy begins its journey into the city. The weight of the evening's events looms over everyone, their fates intertwined in ways most of them have yet to realize.

As the gala venue comes into view, the Mitchells brace themselves for what promises to be a night of revelations, power plays, and unforeseen consequences.

Chapter 3: Act 1 – The Gala

The convoy of black SUVs glides through the bustling streets of downtown Jacksonville, stopping in front of the Times Union Center. Paparazzi cameras flash as the sleek vehicles pull up to the red carpet, and the excitement in the air is palpable. The Mitchell family begins to disembark, their presence commanding attention from the crowd. Mob-Lee steps out of his SUV and adjusts his suit, noticing how it perfectly contrasts with the flashing lights around them. He stands, silently taking in the chaos of the night.

"A lot of eyes on us tonight," Aura-Lee says, coming up beside him. She smirks, looking around at the scene. "You ready for this, Lee?"

Mob-Lee nods but doesn't say anything at first, his thoughts focused elsewhere.

"I'm ready," he finally replies, though the weight of the upcoming presentation presses on him.

Outside, Mob-Lee watches the glamorous event unfold. Celebrities and dignitaries walk the red carpet, smiling for the cameras, surrounded by a buzz of conversation. He feels somewhat out of place amidst the glitter and flash of the high society. He scans the crowd, his eyes flicking from one face to another, none of them as important as the woman he spots across the carpet—Tasha.

Her beauty radiates in an emerald dress that catches the lights as she moves. She laughs at something Brandon Corvin says beside her, and Mob-Lee's chest tightens, the sight of them together sending a wave of anger and longing through him. He quickly looks away, taking a deep breath.

"I shouldn't have come," Mob-Lee mutters under his breath, stepping back into the shadows.

Tasha continues to move down the red carpet, her posture graceful and assured. The way she carries herself, the way she smiles for the cameras, only increases Mob-Lee's internal struggle. He watches her closely, his heart pounding in his chest.

"Hey, Mob-Lee," Aura-Lee says, nudging him with her elbow. "It's fine. You've got this."

Mob-Lee glances over at her, nodding but barely hearing her. His gaze is locked on Tasha. She catches sight of him from across the way, and for just a second, their eyes meet. Mob-Lee feels a spark, an old connection, but before he can react, Brandon steps forward.

"Smile, Tasha," he says, his arm casually going around her waist for a photo op.

Mob-Lee's stomach tightens. He can't stand the sight of them together, but he forces himself to look away.

The crowd parts as a sleek pearl white Bentley pulls up. Destiny Knight, the CEO of Optimized Education, steps out, the cameras capturing her every move. The midnight blue gown she wears hugs her body perfectly, shimmering with silver embroidery that catches the light. Her dark skin glows against the backdrop of the flashing bulbs.

Mob-Lee's eyes widen as he watches her, captivated by her presence.

"Damn," he mutters to himself. "She's... she's something else."

Aura-Lee raises an eyebrow, noticing his reaction. "Focus, Lee. This is about you tonight, not some pretty CEO."

But Mob-Lee can't help but admire her. As she waves to the cameras, he looks down at his suit, noticing how it compliments her gown in a way that feels destined.

"She's the one, huh?" Aura-Lee teases, nudging him.

Mob-Lee snaps back to reality. "I'm not here for that, Aura. Focus."

The Mitchell family makes their grand entrance, the spotlight turning to them as they walk through the doors of the venue. Mob-Lee steps in after them, straightening his tie and inhaling deeply. He can't shake the feeling that this night will change everything. His family's legacy, the business world, and his own future are all on the line.

"You're good, Mob-Lee," Aunt Camille says, her voice low and steady as she passes him. She gives him a reassuring pat on the shoulder. "Remember what we're here for. Just stay focused."

Mob-Lee nods, scanning the room. He's about to head deeper into the venue when he catches sight of Brandon and Tasha again, this time across the room. Brandon's arm is draped casually around her shoulder. The sight sends a wave of anger through Mob-Lee, but he bites it back.

"Stay calm," Mob-Lee whispers to himself. "This is bigger than her. It's bigger than all of them."

He takes a final breath and heads into the crowd, ready for whatever the night holds.

As the guests are checked in and escorted to their tables, the atmosphere inside the venue is alive with excitement and anticipation. The space is beautifully decorated, with elegant chandeliers overhead and tables adorned with white roses and gold trim. The buzz of conversation grows louder as everyone finds their seats, and soon the room falls silent as Destiny Knight steps onto the stage.

She adjusts the microphone, her commanding presence instantly taking control of the room. "Good evening, everyone," she begins, her voice warm but confident. "Thank you for joining us tonight for what promises to be a memorable evening. A special thank you to the Hunter Family Foundation, whose support has been instrumental in all of my success. It's truly a privilege to stand before you tonight."

The crowd erupts in applause as Destiny smiles graciously, giving a nod toward the Hunter family representatives in the front row.

Destiny continues, her voice now softer but filled with purpose. "Optimized Education was founded with a mission to provide cutting-edge, accessible education to children from every walk of life. We aim to empower the next generation of leaders, thinkers, and innovators. But none of this would be possible without the unwavering support of all of you in this room tonight. This gala is not only a celebration but also a call to action—one that will shape the future of education for years to come."

As Destiny speaks, Mob-Lee listens intently, admiring her poise and strength. His mind races, the pressure mounting, but he steadies himself, knowing the time to act is coming soon.

Destiny outlines the evening's schedule with excitement. "Tonight, we have an unforgettable experience prepared for you. A five-course dinner, an auction featuring exclusive and rare items, and the presentation of a groundbreaking merger proposal. We'll also be graced by a special musical guest who will perform later in the evening, and of course, a night of dancing and celebration."

She pauses, letting the words hang in the air before continuing with a smile. "And for the grand raffle tonight, one lucky winner will take home an extraordinary educational experience—an all-expenses-paid scholarship to the most prestigious academic institution of their choice, including travel and living expenses. A once-in-a-lifetime opportunity to further your education in a way that will change your life."

The crowd responds with applause, buzzing with excitement at the prospect of such a grand prize.

Destiny snaps her fingers, and the servers begin to flood the room with the first course—an elegant salad topped with exotic fruits and a tangy vinaigrette. As the servers move from table to table, the atmosphere shifts into one of relaxed enjoyment.

"Aura-Lee," Mob-Lee whispers as he watches the servers glide by. "You were right—this place is beautiful. But I can't help feeling like the weight of the world's on my shoulders right now."

Aura-Lee leans closer, her eyes twinkling. "Take it all in, Lee. Turn the charm on. You've got this."

Mob-Lee smiles, a mischievous glint in his eyes. As the first course is placed in front of him, he leans back in his chair, a confident, relaxed posture, and begins to entertain those around him.

"Did I ever tell you about the time I got kicked out of military school for moonlighting as a DJ?" Mob-Lee asks with a grin, launching into a story that blends humor with his undeniable charm. Laughter erupts around the table, and soon, his anecdotes flow freely, from college pranks to military antics.

He regales the table with a particularly funny tale about how he once tricked an instructor into thinking he'd passed a complex exam when in fact, he had swapped out the answer sheet the night before. The room roars with laughter as Mob-Lee effortlessly steals the spotlight, his quick wit and natural charisma making him the center of attention.

Across the room, Robert Xavier and Vance sit at a nearby table, visibly irritated by the attention Mob-Lee is receiving. Robert narrows his eyes, his grip tightening on his glass. Vance, who shares the frustration, leans in to whisper.

"Damn it, Mob-Lee's got all the attention. This wasn't supposed to be his night."

Robert glances over at the table where Mob-Lee's laughter echoes, his charm impossible to ignore. "He's too damn good at this. Let's go mingle with the others. I'm not sitting here watching him steal the spotlight."

The two exchange a look of frustration before they excuse themselves, making their way toward a group of business associates.

As they leave the table, Mob-Lee catches a brief glimpse of them and grins, unbothered. He knows this is his moment, and no one—especially not Robert and Vance—will take that away from him.

The night is just getting started, and Mob-Lee feels the weight of his decisions settling on his shoulders. He takes another deep breath, ready to face what lies ahead.

Destiny takes a moment to sit at the Hunter family table, her midnight blue gown shimmering under the chandeliers. She leans in to hug Isabel Hunter, who smiles warmly.

"I'm so proud of you," Isabel says softly, her voice full of emotion.

"Thanks, Mom," Destiny replies, her eyes glistening.

Destiny reflects on how Isabel adopted her at 13 after her parents' tragic death. Isabel, unable to conceive, dedicated her life to fostering and adopting, raising 45 children. Her love and guidance have shaped countless lives, and Destiny feels a deep gratitude.

Isabel gives Destiny's hand a gentle squeeze. "Tonight is just the beginning, my dear. The world is watching, and you're shining."

Destiny nods, embracing the encouragement before excusing herself to return to her hosting duties. Isabel watches her leave, her pride evident as Destiny disappears into the bustling gala crowd.

In a secluded corner, Robert Xavier and Vance Cruz huddle with the Black Sky Group board members: Booker Brown, Stanley Davis, and Malcolm Day.

The three men, all seasoned and accomplished businessmen, exude authority. Their reputations command respect.

Robert gestures dramatically, his tone filled with urgency. "This merger will bring Black Sky to the forefront of the industry. And with ValorTech's backing—"

Booker interrupts, his voice laced with skepticism. "That's all well and good, but where's the substance? This feels half-baked."

Stanley Davis leans forward, his expression unyielding. "We've seen ValorTech's support waver in the past. What guarantees do you have?"

Malcolm Day, his voice low but commanding, adds, "If you can't close this deal, don't expect us to clean up your mess."

The tension thickens as Booker rises, straightening his tie. "Gentlemen, I suggest you figure it out. Or be prepared to face the consequences."

Robert and Vance are left seething as the board members walk away.

Destiny steps onto the stage, microphone in hand. "Ladies and gentlemen, it's time for our grand raffle. Get your tickets ready!"

The room hums with anticipation as she pulls a ticket. "The winning number is... 24521!"

Aura-Lee leaps to her feet, waving her ticket excitedly. "That's me!" she exclaims, making her way to the stage as the crowd claps politely.

Mob-Lee cheers from the side, his voice booming. "That's my sister! Let's go!"

Destiny greets Aura-Lee with a warm handshake and hands her the scholarship prize paperwork.

Aura-Lee beams at the crowd. "I'd like to thank my brother Mob-Lee for buying this ticket, because we all know I'm not spending $5,000 on anything that's not an international flight!"

The room erupts in laughter, with several guests clapping harder.

As the laughter settles, Destiny leans in, whispering to Aura-Lee. "If I let you perform now, everyone will think this raffle was rigged."

Aura-Lee chuckles, but instead of backing down, she grabs the microphone.

"Thaaaaaaank yoooooou, thaaank yooou, thank you!" she sings, her voice melodic and soulful. The room falls silent, enraptured by her impromptu performance. Her voice echoes beautifully, capturing every emotion in its notes.

When she finishes, the room erupts in applause, with some standing to cheer. Mob-Lee whistles proudly, his grin wide as he watches his sister bask in the admiration of the crowd.

Destiny takes the microphone once again, her voice professional but warm.

"Thank you, Aura-Lee, for that beautiful moment. And thank you, everyone, for your generosity tonight. Now, as we prepare for the next phase of the evening, feel free to mingle and enjoy yourselves. Presentations will begin shortly."

The crowd begins to shift, conversations and laughter filling the room as servers circulate with drinks.

Mob-Lee watches the scene from a distance, his mind turning to his upcoming presentation. He notices Robert and Vance exchanging hushed, heated words near the corner but decides to stay focused on his own task.

Aura-Lee joins him, nudging his arm. "You're up soon. Turn on the charm and knock 'em dead, little brother."

Mob-Lee nods, straightening his suit. "Always do, sis."

As the room buzzes with excitement and anticipation, the stakes are higher than ever. The evening's drama is only beginning to unfold.

The room darkens, and a stunning visual display fills the massive screens as the presentations begin. The crowd murmurs in awe, captivated by the graphics.

Diane Sterling, a poised young woman in a sleek black gown, takes the stage. "Good evening, everyone. I'm Diane Sterling, representing Obsidian Night."

The crowd leans in as Diane speaks confidently about her family's nightclub chain. "Our vision is simple: merging entertainment and education. By opening our venues to students of the arts, we provide hands-on training in audio engineering, stage production, and performance. This is how we invest in the future of creativity."

Her pitch is seamless, accompanied by visuals of state-of-the-art studios and concert venues. The audience erupts in applause, clearly impressed with her polished delivery and innovative concept.

After several more polished presentations, the crowd's energy shifts as Robert Xavier and Vance Cruz stumble to the stage.

Robert trips slightly, gripping the podium for support as Vance awkwardly clears his throat. "Uh, good evening, everyone," Robert begins, slurring slightly.

The slides are poorly designed, the transitions clunky. Their pitch is disjointed, with Robert mumbling through statistics while Vance interrupts with half-formed thoughts. The audience exchanges glances, some stifling chuckles, others visibly annoyed.

When they finally finish, there's a smattering of polite, half-hearted claps.

As Mob-Lee steps up, he pauses at the podium, a smirk on his face. "My cousins, everyone," he says dryly, earning a wave of laughter.

Mob-Lee's presentation is unlike anything before. Eschewing flashy visuals, he speaks directly to the crowd, his voice steady and commanding. His words flow like a story, captivating the audience. He connects his points to real-world outcomes, painting a vivid picture of the benefits his firm can offer.

"And that," Mob-Lee concludes, "is why Mitchell Global Strategies Firm should be considered for a merger with Optimized Education."

The room is silent for a moment, Thunderous applause erupts. Some are stunned, gasps ripple through the audience. Whispers spread quickly.

"Wait, he's the CEO of thee Global Strategies?" someone mutters.

Tasha's eyes widen as realization sets in—Mob-Lee isn't just an attendee; if Mob-Lee is the CEO then he's now technically her boss. Her stomach churns, regret flickering in her eyes as she glances at Brandon, who looks equally unsettled.

Robert and Vance exchange panicked looks. "How did we not know Global Strategies was family-owned?" Vance whispers furiously.

As Mob-Lee steps off the stage, the crowd explodes into applause again. People rise to their feet, clapping and cheering for over five minutes.

Destiny catches Mob-Lee's attention as she heads toward the stage, her gown gliding effortlessly. "Nice suit," she murmurs, her tone impressed, As she catches the perfect match of fabric and embroidery. The stitching from both of them made the shape of what looked like a rose as they walked by each other.

"Thanks," Mob-Lee replies with a slight smile, walking back to his seat.

Logan claps him on the shoulder as he passes. "Great fucking job, Mob."

At the Mitchell table, Aunt Camille beams with pride, her hands clasped together. Aura-Lee leans in, her voice low but confident. "You just secured that deal, little brother."

Mob-Lee sits down, exhaling deeply, a sense of pride washing over him.

Across the room, Brandon seethes quietly. He had been banking on his partnership with Robert and Vance to further his plans, but Mob-Lee's unexpected gift of gab has thrown everything into disarray.

His jaw tightens as he watches Mob-Lee sit back confidently. The applause is still lingering, and Mob-Lee's name is now on everyone's lips.

Brandon's mind races. His plans are unraveling, and a new obstacle has emerged: Mob-Lee Mitchell.

"Time for a new strategy," Brandon mutters under his breath, his eyes narrowing.

The doors to the gallery swing open, revealing a dazzling display of wealth and culture. The room is bathed in soft golden light, highlighting the treasures within: antiques, rare collectibles, masterful paintings, intricate sculptures, and limited-edition books. Each piece is curated to radiate exclusivity.

As guests file in, conversations buzz with anticipation. Mob-Lee steps in with the Mitchell family, his eyes scanning the room. Aunt Camille's presence beside him is both commanding and comforting. She leans toward him with a sly smile, her voice low and conspiratorial.

"Lil Lee," she begins, holding out a sapphire-colored metal card. "This is your key to the premier account. Two hundred billion dollars."

Mob-Lee blinks, momentarily stunned.

"Tonight," Camille continues, her smile widening, "decorate your space. A blank canvas needs the right masterpiece. Oh, and don't be afraid to stunt on 'em a little. Let them see what Mitchell money really means."

Mob-Lee chuckles, gripping the card. "'Stunt on 'em,' huh?" he repeats, a mischievous glint in his eye.

"I'm serious," she adds, tapping his shoulder. "This crowd? They think they're important. Remind them who they're sitting with."

He nods, tucking the card into his pocket.

Mob-Lee takes his seat near the front, casually spinning the bidding paddle in his hands as he surveys the room. The crowd is a tapestry of prestige: billionaires, dignitaries, collectors, and influencers, all poised for the chance to claim a piece of history.

A light tap on his shoulder interrupts his thoughts. Turning, he locks eyes with Tasha.

"Hey, Mob," she says, her tone casual but with an edge of flirty nervousness. "Long time no see."

Mob-Lee's jaw tightens as a rush of emotions floods him: betrayal, anger, and an ache he can't fully shake. "Yeah," he replies, keeping his voice even. "Long time."

Tasha takes the seat directly behind him, leaning slightly forward. "You look good," she says softly.

Mob-Lee doesn't turn. "Thanks," he says curtly.

From across the room, Brandon notices Tasha's proximity to Mob-Lee. His expression darkens as he watches her lean in.

Brandon grips his paddle tightly, his mind drifting back to the previous night. Tasha's moans echo in his memory: Oh, Mob! The way her voice softened, the way her eyes lit up when she said Mob—it all replays vividly.

His fingers tighten around the paddle as he shakes off the memory. "Focus," he mutters under his breath. But his gaze keeps darting back to Tasha and Mob-Lee.

Mob-Lee, sensing Brandon's stare, smirks to himself. He leans back slightly, just enough to let Brandon know he's aware.

The auctioneer steps to the podium, their voice commanding the room. "Ladies and gentlemen, welcome to tonight's exclusive auction. We begin with a one-of-a-kind 18th-century Ming vase. Starting bid: $10,000."

Paddles shoot up around the room, the numbers climbing rapidly.

Tasha leans forward, her voice low. "That vase would look great in your place."

Mob-Lee glances over his shoulder, his expression stone. "You think so?"

Tasha shrugs, her tone dripping with flirtation. "Just a thought."

The bidding continues, and Mob-Lee keeps his paddle lowered, watching as the price soars to $50,000. The room grows tense as two bidders go head-to-head.

As the next item is unveiled—an original painting by a renowned artist—Aunt Camille watches Mob-Lee closely.

"Don't wait too long," she whispers as she passes by his seat. "Make your move when it counts."

Mob-Lee smiles, gripping the sapphire card in his pocket. The auctioneer announces the next item: a 19th-century clock crafted by a French artisan, starting at $15,000.

Mob-Lee raises his paddle. The room shifts its attention to him.

"fifteen thousand," he says confidently.

The auctioneer nods. "fifteen thousand, to bidder 21."

Another paddle goes up. "Twenty-five thousand."

Mob-Lee raises his again. "Thirty."

The crowd murmurs, intrigued by his boldness. Aunt Camille smirks from her seat, while Robert Xavier and Vance exchange uneasy glances.

The bidding escalates, but Mob-Lee remains calm, finally securing the clock at $50,000. The room applauds lightly as the auctioneer hammers the sale.

As Mob-Lee sits back, Tasha leans closer. "Nice purchase," she says softly. Running her hand across his shoulder.

He turns, locking eyes with her for a moment. "Thanks."

Across the room, Brandon seethes, his plans unraveling further. He watches as Mob-Lee begins to dominate the room's attention, his confidence growing with each bid.

The tension in the gallery is real, as the auction continues, each item bringing new stakes and higher bids. Mob-Lee, now fully in his element, knows the night is just beginning.

The gallery hums with quiet excitement as staff meticulously arrange the centerpiece of the evening: the Black Forever Collection, a series of exquisite jewelry pieces shrouded in mystique and unmatched craftsmanship. A brief intermission allows the crowd to mingle.

Tasha, lingering near Mob-Lee, lets her voice carry just enough to pique his interest. "That collection is breathtaking," she says, her eyes fixed on the display being unveiled. "The ring… it's perfect."

Mob-Lee raises an eyebrow, his interest piqued by her intentional comment. "Noted," he says smoothly, a hint of mischief curling at his lips as he steps away.

Moments later, Brandon corners Tasha, his tone sharp. "What's going on with you and the Mitchell brat?"

Tasha rolls her eyes. "Nothing. I just complimented his presentation earlier."

Brandon leans closer, his voice dropping. "It looked like more than that."

Tasha waves him off. "You're paranoid," she says coolly, but Brandon's jaw tightens, his gaze lingering on Mob-Lee across the room.

The auction resumes, and the Black Forever Collection is finally revealed, eliciting gasps from the crowd. Each piece is unique, shimmering under the gallery lights. The starting bid for each item is announced: $500,000.

Brandon glances at Tasha, determination etched into his face. *I'll get her something she won't forget.* He's set a budget of $5 million, convinced it will be enough to win the bid and win her over.

The first item—a stunning diamond necklace—immediately sparks competition. Mob-Lee raises his paddle with calm precision, his expression cool and collected. Brandon follows suit, and the two lock into an unspoken rivalry. After raising the bid and other bidders dropping out its down to Brandon and Mob-Lee.

"Five million," Brandon declares, his voice steady.

"Six," Mob-Lee counters without hesitation.

The auctioneer's gavel falls, and Mob-Lee secures the necklace.

This pattern continues, item after item. Brandon's frustration grows as Mob-Lee outbids him every time, effortlessly surpassing the $5 million limit Brandon refuses to cross.

Finally, the pièce de résistance is unveiled: a 10-carat black diamond ring, the crown jewel of the collection.

"Starting bid: $1,000,000," the auctioneer announces.

Brandon leans forward, his paddle raised. "One million."

"Two," Mob-Lee counters smoothly.

The bids climb rapidly, the room captivated by the battle between the two men.

"Five million," Brandon says, his voice tense.

"Six," Mob-Lee replies, his tone casual, as if the money were inconsequential.

Brandon, desperate to win, clenches his jaw. "Seven point five."

Mob-Lee pauses, then lets his paddle drop. "All yours," he says with a faint chuckle.

A wave of whispers ripples through the crowd as Brandon sits back, triumphant yet uneasy. He quickly realizes the cost of his "victory"— he's exceeded his budget.

As the auction concludes and deals are finalized, Brandon is forced to forfeit the ring to Mob-Lee, As one of the administrators tells him the house rules. Any bid that is finalized as sold but the bidder is unable to settle the balance the item shall be available to the next highest bidder at the amount of their last bid. Brandon's face burns with humiliation as he excuses himself from the gallery.

Mob-Lee, calm and collected, begins distributing his winnings. He hands a jewelry box to Aura-Lee. "This will look great on you," he says warmly.

To Aunt Camille, he presents a bracelet from the collection. "For everything you've done," he says.

A vintage pocket watch is given to Logan. "Figured you'd appreciate this," Mob-Lee quips.

Finally, Tasha approaches him, her tone playful yet curious. "So, which one is mine?"

Mob-Lee smirks, his response cutting. "The one Brandon bought you."

Her face falters as she processes his words. Before she can reply, Mob-Lee turns away, leaving her in stunned silence.

Destiny gathers the remaining crowd to announce the winner of the merger proposal. "Ladies and gentlemen, the decision has been made. The winner is… Mob-Lee Mitchell of Mitchell Global Strategies Firm!"

The room erupts into applause. Aura-Lee beams, nudging Mob-Lee. "A three-way Mitchell sweep," she says proudly.

Robert and Vance slip out of the gallery, their expressions dark as they hastily exit.

Brandon, on the other hand, lingers in the corner, a storm of emotions brewing. Embarrassment, rage, and betrayal swirl within him as he watches the Mitchells revel in their triumph.

As the guests begin to leave, Mob-Lee hangs back to chat with Destiny. After a few minutes, he excuses himself to the restroom.

Inside, Brandon is waiting.

"Good job in there," Brandon says, his voice dripping with sarcasm.

Mob-Lee raises an eyebrow, drying his hands. "Thanks," he replies nonchalantly.

Brandon steps closer, his fists clenched. "You think you're better than me, don't you?"

Mob-Lee remains calm, his gaze unwavering. "who the fuck are you?"

Brandon's jaw tightens, his body language signaling a brewing confrontation. The tension in the air is thick, crackling with the promise of violence.

Mob-Lee, sensing what's coming, smirks. "You sure you want to do this here?"

Brandon steps even closer, his voice a low growl. "You've been asking for this all night."

Chapter 4 Brawling

The bathroom is eerily silent, save for the subtle hum of fluorescent lights. Mob-Lee and Brandon stand inches apart, the tension palpable. Mob-Lee's sharp gaze locks on Brandon's smug expression, waiting for the inevitable clash.

Just then, faint laughter drifts through the hallway outside, followed by Tasha's unmistakable voice. Brandon freezes for a moment before straightening his suit jacket.

"Another time, Mitchell," he mutters, his voice dripping with disdain. Without a second glance, he exits the bathroom, the door swinging shut behind him.

Brandon catches up to Tasha, plastering on a faux smile as they walk together. As they near his security detail, he leans into one guard whispering something inaudible, followed by a subtle signal toward the bathroom.

Four men from his detail peel off, heading toward the restroom. The two remaining guards escort Brandon and Tasha toward an awaiting black SUV, engines purring softly.

Inside the Bathroom Mob-Lee exhales, turning toward the mirror. He splashes water on his face, the cool sensation grounding him as he reflects on the evening's success. His lips curl into a grin, savoring his victory over Brandon at the auction

The door creaks open behind him. Mob-Lee glances up, meeting the reflection of four tailored enforcers in the mirror. The last man shuts the door, twisting the lock with an ominous click.

Mob-Lee sighs, casually slipping out of his tailored jacket and hanging it on a nearby hook in one fluid motion. He turns to face them, rolling his shoulders, a faint smirk playing on his lips.

'Don't want to get blood on my new suit. I think she liked it," he quips, his tone light but his eyes sharp, assessing each man's stance

One of the men steps forward, his voice a low growl. "Mr. Corvin sends his regards.

Without warning, the thug charges

Mob-Lee sidesteps gracefully, using the man's momentum against him. He hooks his arm around the thug's neck, spinning him off balance and driving a knee into his nose with a sickening crack. The man collapses to the floor, blood pouring from his shattered face.

Mob-Lee glances down at his pants, inspecting near his knee. "Close call," he mutters, relieved to see no stains.

The remaining three hesitate briefly before two rush in simultaneously. One wields a retractable baton, its metallic snap echoing in the small space

The man swings wide, but Mob-Lee ducks under the arc, delivering a lightning-quick jab to the attacker's throat. The thug staggers back, clutching his neck as he gasps for air.

The second man takes advantage of Mob-Lee's focus, landing a heavy blow to the back of his head. Staggered but not deterred, Mob-Lee drops low, spinning with a sweeping kick that knocks the man off his feet.

Before the thug can recover, Mob-Lee pounces dragging him up by the collar and unleashing a barrage of brutal punches to his face. Blood spatters across the floor as the man slumps into unconsciousness, Mob-Lee's fists slowing only when his target stops moving.

Breathing heavily, Mob-Lee looks up, his eyes locking onto the fourth and final man.

The remaining thug, frozen in the corner, hesitates. His eyes dart to the locked door, then back to Mob-Lee, calculating his chances

Mob-Lee exhales sharply, smoothing his tie and retrieving his jacket. His movements are calm, deliberate, and terrifyingly controlled

"When you wake your friends up," he says, his voice cold and unwavering, "tell them Mob-Lee says, 'no more locked doors.'"

The thug stumbles toward the door, fumbling with the lock before yanking it open. He steps aside as Mob-Lee strides out, adjusting his jacket as if nothing happened.

the wreckage left behind: three bloodied, unconscious men sprawled across the tiled floor, the fourth trembling as he locks eyes with his defeated comrades.

The door swings shut behind Mob-Lee, leaving only silence in its wake.

Brandon's SUV glides through the city streets, a tense silence filling the cabin. Tasha stares out the window, her reflection a picture of unease. Brandon's expression is distant, his thoughts hidden behind the storm brewing in his mind.

Finally, Brandon speaks, his voice sharp and demanding.

"So, how do you know him?" He doesn't bother looking at her. "And don't lie to me, Tasha. I saw how you looked at him tonight."

Tasha hesitates, her fingers twisting the strap of her designer purse. "We... dated," she admits reluctantly. "During our last two years in college. Up until a few months ago, when you and I..."

"Really?" Brandon interrupts, his voice dripping with venom. "So, while you were with me, you were still thinking about him?"

Tasha shakes her head, defensive. "No! I wasn't. Mob-Lee and I were over before you and I got serious."

Brandon leans forward, his elbows on his knees, his frustration barely contained. "Did you know who he really is?"

"What do you mean?" Tasha asks cautiously.

Brandon's lips curl into a bitter smile. "The company you work for? Global Strategies? It's actually Mitchell Global Strategies Firm. You didn't think it was weird?"

Tasha's jaw tightens. "I knew, but it didn't matter. It's a job, Brandon. That's all it was."

Brandon leans back, the gears in his mind turning. Tasha's words provide little comfort, but the satisfaction of having "won" her from Mob-Lee keeps his rage in check—for now.

In the backseat of another SUV, Mob-Lee leans back, rubbing the tender spot on the back of his head.

"That little bitch got me good," he mutters with a smirk, the absurdity of the situation coaxing a chuckle out of him.

The city lights fade as the vehicle approaches the Mitchell Estate. Mob-Lee gazes out the window, his thoughts replaying the evening. The tense auction, Brandon's weak attempts at bravado, and, of course, Tasha's conflicted glances.

Yet, it's not Tasha who lingers in his mind the most—it's Destiny. Her confidence, her poise, and that subtle yet unmistakable interest she showed in him.

As the estate looms into view, his phone buzzes. He glances at the screen, raising an eyebrow at the unknown number. Opening the message, he reads:

"It was a pleasure meeting you this evening. I hung around with hopes to chat, but you seemed to have left. Anyways, congrats—and that was a very nice suit. -DKnight"

A grin spreads across Mob-Lee's face. "Interesting," he murmurs, tucking the phone away as the SUV pulls through the gates.

Brandon's SUV pulls into the circular driveway of their hotel. He exits first, his security detail trailing closely behind. Tasha follows reluctantly, her thoughts a tangled web of guilt and curiosity.

Brandon pauses at the entrance, his eyes cold as he whispers something to one of his guards. The man nods and walks away, his destination unclear.

Inside the elevator, Tasha finally speaks. "What's your problem, Brandon? Are you seriously jealous of Mob-Lee?"

Brandon scoffs. "Jealous? No. But I don't trust him, and neither should you. He's not who you think he is, Tasha. Trust me."

Tasha crosses her arms, but the doubt in her eyes betrays her. "You don't know him like I do."

Brandon leans in, his voice low and threatening. "No, but I know enough to handle him. And I will."

The elevator dings, and they step out, each consumed by their own thoughts.

The Mitchell Estate glows softly under the moonlight as Mob-Lee steps out of the SUV. The vast property, with its sprawling lawns and stately mansion, feels surreal.

As he enters, Aura-Lee greets him with a warm smile. "Long night?"

"You could say that," Mob-Lee replies, running a hand across his head.

Aura-Lee notices the faint bruise forming on the back of his head. "What happened to you?"

"Let's just say Brandon Corvin has got a creative way of saying goodbye," Mob-Lee quips, his tone light.

Aura-Lee shakes her head. "You should be careful, Mob. People like him don't play fair."

"Fair?" Mob-Lee smirks. "Sis, you know me better than that. Fair's not my style either."

Mob-Lee sits in his room, the events of the evening replaying in his mind. He pulls out his phone, rereading Destiny's message.

The door creaks open, and Logan steps in. "How'd it go after?"

"Eventful," Mob-Lee says, slipping his phone back into his pocket.

Logan nods. "Brandon's not done with you, you know."

"I'd be disappointed if he was," Mob-Lee replies with a smirk.

Logan chuckles. "Get some rest, kid. Tomorrow's another day."

As the door closes, Mob-Lee leans back in his chair, a steely determination settling over him. The game has only just begun.

The silence of the east wing is shattered by Camille Mitchell's voice echoing over the intercom.

"Robert. Vance. Get your asses to my study immediately."

Robert groans, rolling out of bed, his head pounding from last night's indulgences. Across the hall, Vance stumbles out of his room, equally disheveled. They lock eyes, both dreading what's to come.

"She's pissed," Robert mutters, rubbing his temples.

"Yeah, no shit," Vance replies, pulling on a wrinkled shirt.

They trudge toward the west wing, each step heavier than the last. The ornate double doors to Camille's study loom ahead, an unspoken promise of hell.

"Close the fucking door," Camille snaps the moment they enter.

The brothers exchange uneasy glances before obeying. Camille stands behind her massive mahogany desk, her piercing gaze cutting through them like a blade.

"What the hell is wrong with you two?" she begins, her voice icy yet furious.

She berates them relentlessly—first for their drunken antics at the gala, then for their lack of decorum and competence during the presentation. Finally, she slams her hand on the desk, her expression darkening.

"And now I hear you've been dealing with Brandon Corvin. Do you two have any idea what you're playing with?"

Robert shifts uncomfortably. "It's business, mom. That's all."

"Business?" Camille spits, her tone venomous. "The Corvins aren't business partners—they're blood enemies. There's a feud between our families that spans decades. And now you've handed him ammunition against us."

Vance attempts to speak, but Camille silences him with a raised hand. "Fix it. Both of you. Or I'll personally see to it that you're cut off—financially and otherwise."

Her words hang heavy in the air. Robert and Vance nod solemnly before retreating from the study, the door closing behind them with a foreboding thud.

Hours later, Robert and Vance sit in the backseat of a luxury sedan, the city blurring past them. Their phones vibrate incessantly—calls from Brandon Corvin—but neither bothers to answer.

"What's the plan?" Vance finally asks, breaking the tense silence.

"We need to regain control," Robert says, his jaw clenched. "And fast."

Their destination comes into view: the sleek, imposing headquarters of Black Sky Group. At the entrance, Brandon Corvin waits with Booker Brown, the senior board member of Black Sky. The sight of them sends a shiver of unease down both men's spines.

The executive conference room buzzes with anger and frustration. Board members shout over one another, their voices a cacophony of rage. Robert and Vance sit stiffly at the table, flanked by Brandon and his team from ValorTech.

"This mess is on you two!" one board member shouts, pointing an accusatory finger. "You promised results, and instead, you've brought us to the brink of collapse!"

Robert's fists clench under the table, but he stays silent. Vance glares at the speaker, but before he can retort, Brandon rises from his chair.

"Enough," Brandon says coldly, holding up a document. "Here's what you need to understand. The contract you failed to secure has consequences."

He places the paper on the table, his smile sharp and predatory. "As per this agreement, ValorTech now holds a majority share of Black Sky Group—51% to be exact."

The room erupts into chaos. Board members shout threats and accusations, their faces red with anger.

"You've destroyed us!" one cries. "Our jobs, our families—gone, all because of your incompetence!"

Brandon remains unfazed, his calm demeanor only fueling the rage around him. He waits for the noise to die down before delivering the final blow.

"As of now, Black Sky Group is under my control," he announces. "Effective immediately, Booker Brown, Stanley Davis, Malcolm Day, and their personal assistants are terminated. Collect your things and leave the premises."

The named individuals stare in shock before reluctantly rising and exiting the room. Booker glares at Robert and Vance on his way out, his expression promising retribution.

Robert and Vance sit in stunned silence as the room empties, leaving only them and Brandon. The air feels heavy, suffocating.

Brandon glances at his watch. "You two. Booker's old office. Now."

Without waiting for a response, he strides out, leaving them to follow like chastised children.

They enter the office minutes later, the space eerily quiet without its former occupant. Brandon stands by the window, gazing out at the city below.

"Do you know why I keep winning?" he asks without turning around.

Robert stiffens. "Because you cheat."

Brandon chuckles darkly. "No, Robert. Because I'm always two steps ahead." He finally turns to face them, his smile cold and menacing. "And you? You're already out of moves."

As Robert and Vance leave the office, their expressions grim, a sense of dread settles over them. Brandon's words echo in their minds, a chilling reminder of how precarious their position has become.

Meanwhile, back at the Mitchell Estate, Camille watches the scene unfold on a secure feed. Her fingers drum against the armrest of her chair, her expression unreadable.

"Let's see how far they'll fall before they beg for help," she murmurs.

The pieces are in motion, but the game is far from over.

The midday sun glints off the water as Mob-Lee drives southward across the Dames Point Bridge, the city's skyline fading in his rearview mirror. His phone rings, and the car's Bluetooth system automatically answers.

"Hello," Mob-Lee says, his tone neutral yet curious.

"Hello, Mr. Mitchell," a warm, familiar voice replies. "This is Destiny Knight."

Mob-Lee sits up straighter, a small smile tugging at his lips. "Hi, Ms. Knight."

"I was wondering if I could treat you to lunch soon," Destiny says, her voice smooth and confident.

Mob-Lee grins. "I could eat."

"How about today? Morton's by the river?" she suggests.

Mob-Lee glances at the clock on the dashboard—12:45 PM. "Sounds good. What time?"

"1:30," Destiny answers.

"Perfect. I'll see you there."

Ending the call, Mob-Lee quickly inputs "Morton's" into his navigation system. The route directs him to the Hyatt Regency. With the clock ticking, he accelerates.

Arriving just before 1:30 PM, Mob-Lee pulls up to the Hyatt Regency's valet station. Handing over his keys, he straightens his blazer and steps inside. The elegant interior of Morton's is filled with the soft hum of conversation and the clinking of glasses.

At a window seat overlooking the serene river, Destiny Knight sits waiting, her confident posture and radiant smile instantly catching his eye.

Mob-Lee approaches, extending his hand. "Pleasure to formally meet you, Ms. Knight."

"Please, call me Destiny," she replies, her handshake firm yet warm.

Mob-Lee smiles. "Destiny it is."

The two settle into their conversation, the hours slipping by unnoticed. They delve into stories about their childhoods, sharing laughs and memories. The conversation shifts to the gala, where Mob-Lee praises her grace under pressure, and finally to the upcoming merger between Global Strategies and Optimized Education.

"I officially take over as CEO on September 30th," Mob-Lee informs her. "Once that happens, we can finalize the merger."

Destiny nods, impressed. "That's excellent news. I've been reviewing the potential synergies—it's going to be groundbreaking."

As the conversation winds down, Destiny rises from her seat and moves to hug Mob-Lee. The gesture catches him off guard, but he returns the embrace warmly.

"You smell good," they both say simultaneously, laughing at the coincidence.

Destiny waves as the valet pulls her car around. Mob-Lee watches her drive off, his mind still lingering on their meeting.

As Mob-Lee waits for his car, he gazes out over the bustling street. The moment of peace is disrupted when he notices a familiar figure exiting the Hyatt Regency's front doors.

Tasha.

She walks with the same confidence that once captivated him, her designer heels clicking against the pavement. For a fleeting moment, he's transported back to when they were together—her laughter, her touch, her betrayal.

But the spell is broken when Brandon Corvin steps out behind her, placing a hand on her lower back as they approach a waiting car.

Mob-Lee's jaw tightens, but he doesn't move, his emotions warring within him.

As the car pulls away, Mob-Lee exhales slowly, his focus sharpening. He retrieves his car from the valet and heads back toward the northside.

Driving through the city, Mob-Lee reflects on the day. Destiny's warmth, her genuine interest, and her drive feel like a breath of fresh air compared to the complicated history with Tasha.

The sight of her with Brandon stings, but it's a wake-up call. He knows now that the past can't hold him back—his future is far too promising.

"Focus," he mutters to himself, gripping the steering wheel tighter. "There's no time for distractions."

The Dames Point Bridge reappears as he heads back toward the Mitchell Estate, the sunset painting the horizon in shades of orange and gold.

As Mob-Lee arrives at the estate, the sight of its grand architecture no longer overwhelms him. Instead, it fuels his resolve. The stakes are higher than ever, and with the merger, his new role, and the shadows of his past threatening to resurface, he knows he must be ready for whatever comes next.

Stepping out of the car, he heads inside, his mind already formulating his next moves. Destiny's parting words echo in his mind, grounding him:

"Change the game."

With renewed determination, Mob-Lee prepares to take on the challenges ahead, knowing that this is only the beginning.

In a sprawling beachfront mansion, Diane Sterling paces furiously in her high-ceilinged living room, the sound of waves crashing outside doing little to calm her rage.

"How dare that little nobody beat me!" she exclaims, throwing a crystal glass of wine into the fireplace. Her assistant, a wiry man named Edgar, flinches but remains silent.

"Call everyone," Diane snaps, her tone ice-cold. "I want every resource we have digging into Mob-Lee Mitchell and Global Strategies. Family, finances, secrets, I want it all. I don't care how long it takes or how much it costs. Nothing stays hidden from me. And get me 24-hour surveillance on him. If he so much as sneezes, I want to know about it."

"Yes, ma'am," Edgar replies, hurrying out of the room to set her orders in motion.

Diane sinks into an armchair, her manicured fingers gripping the armrests. Her gaze is steely as she mutters to herself, "This isn't over, Mitchell. Not by a long shot."

On the other side of town, the White family gathers in their stately beachfront library. The room is dimly lit, with oak-paneled walls adorned with oil portraits of stern-looking ancestors.

Stanley White, the patriarch, sits at the head of a long table, his hands clasped in front of him. His face is lined with years of disdain and bitterness, and his voice carries a low growl as he speaks.

"That gala was a damn joke," Stanley says. "A circus. I remember when those people knew their place in society. Now they parade around like they own the damn world."

His wife, Eleanor, nods in agreement. "It's disgraceful, Stanley. Disgraceful."

Stanley slams his hand on the table, silencing the room. "It's time for the Whites to rise again. We've been too quiet, too complacent. This city is ours, and we'll take it back. It's time to remind everyone of their place."

"What's the plan, Dad?" asks his eldest son, Grant, his eyes gleaming with excitement.

Stanley leans forward, his voice dropping to a near whisper. "We'll start with the Mitchells. They're the biggest threat. I want everything we can find on them. And when the time comes, we'll strike. Let's make Jacksonville great again."

The family nods in unison, a sinister determination filling the room.

At the Mitchell Estate, Mob-Lee and Aura-Lee lounge in the north wing, surrounded by plush furniture and a massive television. The siblings are relaxed, their laughter filling the room as they toss around ideas for their upcoming 25th birthday party and the merger celebration.

"We need a theme," Aura-Lee says, scrolling through her tablet. "Something classy but fun. How about 'Gatsby meets modern elegance'?"

Mob-Lee chuckles. "Sounds expensive."

Aura-Lee grins. "Good thing we can afford it."

The lighthearted mood shifts as Aura-Lee leans back and sighs. "This is going to get crazy fast. Do you think we're ready for all of this? The merger, the family's expectations, the pressure?"

Mob-Lee's expression turns serious. "No, we're not ready," he admits. "But we weren't made to fail, sis. So we won't fail. Whatever comes our way, we'll handle it."

Aura-Lee smiles, her brother's confidence reassuring her. "You always know what to say, Lee."

Unbeknownst to Mob-Lee and Aura-Lee, enemies are closing in on all sides.

In her home office, Diane Sterling reviews surveillance photos of Mob-Lee, her lips curling into a wicked smile. She picks up her phone and dials a number. "I have some interesting information. Let's meet tomorrow to discuss how we can use it."

Meanwhile, Stanley White pours over old records of the Mitchell family, his mind working on a plan to discredit them publicly. "If we can tarnish their name, we can weaken their influence," he mutters to himself.

Even Brandon Corvin, sitting in his penthouse suite, is plotting his next move. "The Mitchells are going to regret stepping into my world," he says to himself, sipping his whiskey.

The weeks pass in a blur of preparation and planning for the Mitchell siblings. The estate buzzes with activity as staff organize the dual celebration. Invitations are sent, decorations are finalized, and the anticipation builds.

On the eve of their 25th birthday and the merger, Mob-Lee stands on the balcony of the estate, looking out over the sprawling grounds. Aura-Lee joins him, holding two glasses of champagne.

"To us," she says, handing him a glass.

"To us," Mob-Lee echoes, clinking his glass against hers.

As they sip their drinks, a sense of foreboding settles over them. They both know the days ahead will test them like never before.

"We've got this," Mob-Lee says, his voice steady.

Aura-Lee nods, though her grip tightens on the glass. "We don't have a choice."

The siblings standing side by side, the weight of their legacy and the challenges ahead pressing down on them as the clock ticks toward midnight.

Chapter 5 - Day party

The day of the Mitchell twins' 25th birthday dawned bright and clear. Mob-Lee and Aura-Lee had decided to keep their morning lighthearted, letting the chaos of the evening celebration wait its turn. Instead of preparing in silence, they rented a lavish party bus and invited a small entourage of friends and cousins for a day of indulgence.

The festivities started with breakfast and mimosas, laughter ringing out as the bus cruised through downtown Jacksonville. By brunch, they were already tipsy, singing off-key to classics blasting through the bus's speakers.

When lunch rolled around, Mob-Lee stood at the edge of the bus steps, shouting, "I declare the first-ever Mitchell Conga Line!" to the cheers of onlookers. He led the procession with his plate in hand, grinning as strangers joined in along the way.

They decided on an impromptu picnic at Memorial Park, but Mob-Lee had other plans. At Aura-Lee's instruction, the driver veered off the road and onto the park's grass, turning the peaceful green space into a full-blown outdoor club. A portable speaker system blared upbeat tracks, and passersby couldn't resist joining the fun.

Mob-Lee and Aura-Lee passed out shots, grinning as strangers toasted alongside them. The park pulsed with energy, the twins transforming it into the heartbeat of the city.

Destiny Knight, on her way to another errand, couldn't ignore the spectacle. As her car crawled through Riverside, she caught sight of the crowd and immediately recognized Mob-Lee and Aura-Lee, their faces flushed with joy and the buzz of the moment. She pulled over, curious, her reserved demeanor giving way to intrigue.

Destiny approached the scene, weaving through the wobbling crowd performing the Cha Cha Slide. When she finally reached Mob-Lee, her voice cut through the music.

"Hey, Mob!"

The shortening of his name caught him off guard, but the mimosas had loosened him up. Without hesitation, Mob-Lee grabbed her hands, spinning her to the rhythm.

The world seemed to slow for Destiny. For a fleeting moment, it was just her and Mob-Lee, their laughter blending seamlessly with the music.

As the spin ended, Mob-Lee dipped her low and, on a whim, kissed her. It was bold, impulsive, and utterly unexpected. Pulling back with a grin, he declared, "It's my birthday!"

Destiny, stunned but not opposed, blinked before softly replying, "Happy birthday."

Aura-Lee appeared just in time, laughing as she handed Destiny a shot. "It's my birthday too!"

The three toasted, the shot burning smooth as the conversation naturally flowed.

"So, what's the plan for tonight?" Destiny asked, curiosity laced in her voice.

Aura-Lee winked. "You got an invite! It's a Harlem Renaissance theme. Think glitz, glam, and timeless elegance."

"I'll be in burgundy," Mob-Lee added confidently, his mischievous smile leaving an impression.

Destiny nodded, her mind already spinning. As Mob-Lee turned his attention back to the party, Destiny discreetly texted her assistant:

"Find a burgundy dress for tonight. Needs to be at my door by 7 PM."

Hours passed in a blur of laughter, music, and mingling. As the sun began to dip below the horizon, Destiny reluctantly admitted she had called an Uber.

"Stay," Mob-Lee said, offering to take her back on the party bus.

She smiled, touched by the gesture but firm in her decision. "I'll pick up my car tomorrow. Besides, you have a big night ahead."

As her Uber pulled up, Destiny hesitated for a moment, looking at Mob-Lee. "I'll see you tonight, birthday boy."

He grinned. "Count on it."

Destiny slipped into the car, her thoughts lingering on the day's unexpected twists.

The party bus roared back to the Mitchell Estate, the twins and their entourage readying themselves for the evening's grand celebration. As Mob-Lee stepped off the bus, he felt a mix of excitement and anticipation.

The day had been unforgettable, but something about the night ahead felt electric.

In his mind, he replayed the kiss with Destiny, wondering what the evening might bring. With a determined smirk, he strode toward his wing of the mansion, ready to transform for the biggest party of the year.

The anticipation for the evening hung thick in the air, as the Mitchells prepared to set the city ablaze once again.

Mob-Lee entered the master bedroom of his suite, momentarily taken aback by the elaborate decorations. A cascade of balloons filled the corners of the room, shimmering in hues of burgundy and gold, the Mitchell family crest subtly embossed on a few. Gifts were stacked neatly in a corner, ranging from small, ornately wrapped boxes to larger, conspicuously branded packages.

On the edge of the bed sat a sleek tray holding a bottle of 25-year-aged cognac and a single glass. A handwritten note read: "For your 25th. Enjoy the moment. Love, Aunt Camille."

As he took in the room, his phone buzzed, a video call from Aura-Lee lighting up the screen.

"Brooooooo!" she sang dramatically as her face filled the screen. She spun her camera around, revealing her own room, similarly adorned in balloons and gifts.

"Happy birthday, Lee!" she said with exaggerated cheer. "I'm so happy you're back home. This is the best birthday ever!"

Mob-Lee chuckled, her infectious energy lifting his spirits. "Right back at you, sis. Glad we're together again."

She blew a kiss into the camera before abruptly ending the call, likely off to stir up some more birthday antics.

Mob-Lee had just begun tearing into his pile of presents when a firm knock echoed through the room. Crossing to the door, he opened it to find Logan, the family's stoic and ever-reliable guard, standing there.

"Happy birthday, Lil' Lee," Logan said, his gruff tone laced with affection. In his hand, he held a small velvet box.

Mob-Lee tilted his head. "What's this?"

Logan's expression didn't change. "It was your father's."

The words hit Mob-Lee like a freight train. He stood frozen, staring at the tiny box. Slowly, he reached out and took it, the weight of it feeling far heavier than its size.

Opening the box, Mob-Lee's breath caught. Inside was a gold ring with a lion's head, its face encrusted with diamonds that glittered under the room's light.

He remembered the ring vividly, the way it had gleamed on his father's hand when he was a child. Memories of his father's commanding presence flooded his mind—both awe-inspiring and intimidating.

Slipping the ring onto his finger, Mob-Lee felt a mix of emotions—pride, longing, and an unsettling mystery about why this heirloom was being passed to him now.

Before he could speak, Logan handed him an envelope, its wax seal bearing the Mitchell crest.

"From your parents," Logan said simply.

Mob-Lee's heart raced as he stared at the envelope, the seal unbroken.

"Open it after the ceremony," Logan added, turning to leave. He paused at the door, glancing back. "Enjoy the night, Lil' Lee. Your parents always knew you'd make it here."

With that, he was gone.

Across the estate, Logan repeated the process with Aura-Lee, presenting her with a velvet box containing a ring that once belonged to their mother. The delicate band, adorned with sapphires and diamonds, brought tears to her eyes.

"This is..." she whispered, her voice catching.

Logan handed her a wax-sealed envelope as well, the same instruction following. "Open it after the ceremony."

Aura-Lee nodded, watching as Logan exited her room. A deep curiosity swirled in her mind, mingling with emotions she hadn't fully unpacked.

Back in his room, Mob-Lee stared at the envelope for a long moment before setting it aside on his desk. He returned to the pile of gifts, unwrapping them with renewed focus. Each gift was lavish but practical—a luxury watch, high-tech gadgets, custom-tailored suits.

One package stood out: a simple card tucked into a black envelope. Opening it, he read Aunt Camille's note:

"What do you buy for the man who can buy anything he wants? Happy birthday, Leeky. Love, Cammy."

Mob-Lee smirked, shaking his head. "Classic Cam Cam."

As the weight of the moment settled in, Mob-Lee took a deep breath. The ring on his finger felt foreign but comforting, a tangible connection to his past. He glanced at the envelope again but resisted the urge to open it early, choosing instead to focus on the night ahead.

Stepping into his bathroom, he began to clean up, meticulously grooming and preparing himself for the Harlem Renaissance-themed celebration. His burgundy suit awaited him, custom-tailored and perfectly pressed.

Tonight wasn't just a party. It was a statement.

For Mob-Lee Mitchell, the future was wide open—but the shadows of his family's past loomed just behind him, growing closer with every step forward.

The evening air carried an electric charge as the city braced itself for the merger celebration of the decade. Every corner seemed alive with excitement, tension, and a touch of mystery.

At the sprawling Sterling estate, Diane paced her room like a caged tiger. Her personal stylist fussed with the final adjustments on her sequined flapper gown, its gold accents shimmering under the soft glow of her vanity lights.

"Do you think they'll take me seriously tonight?" Diane asked sharply, her voice cutting through the room.

Her assistant, Edgar, nodded hurriedly. "Of course, ma'am. You're Diane Sterling—tonight is your chance to remind them who truly holds the reins in this city."

Diane stopped pacing, her piercing gaze fixed on her reflection. "Good. Because after tonight, they'll know exactly what happens when you cross a Sterling."

In the background, a line of black cars waited in the driveway, their engines humming softly.

Across town, the Hunter family gathered in the parlor of their historic mansion. Jacob Hunter, the patriarch, adjusted the pocket square in his pinstripe suit, his expression stoic.

"This isn't just a party," Jacob said, addressing his wife. "This is an opportunity. Destiny will need us to keep the balance. Remember that."

His wife, Isabel, dressed in a sleek black gown adorned with pearl accents, raised her glass of champagne. "Here's to alliances," she said coolly.

They shared a knowing look before stepping into their waiting limousine.

At the White family estate near the beach, Stanley White poured himself a neat glass of bourbon, staring out at the crashing waves. His wife, Eleanor, entered the room, her jeweled headpiece glinting in the dim light.

"You're brooding again," she said lightly, placing a hand on his shoulder.

Stanley turned to her, his expression grim. "This celebration is nothing more than a charade. The Mitchells think they can waltz in and take over."

Eleanor sighed, adjusting the drape of her shimmering gown. "Stanley, we've survived worse. Just play the part tonight."

Stanley smirked darkly. "Oh, I intend to."

Their son, Grant, stepped in, buttoning his tuxedo jacket. "Let's go show them who really runs this city."

The family strode out, their chauffeur holding the car door open as they climbed into their classic Rolls Royce.

At their sleek downtown headquarters, former members of the Black Sky Group gathered in a private lounge, their tailored suits and vintage gowns exuding wealth and power.

"What's the play tonight?" Malcolm Day asked, lighting a cigar.

"The Mitchells seem to be consolidating power," Stanley Davis replied. "We need to make sure we're positioned to capitalize on their success—or their failure."

The group shared a round of drinks, their conversation laced with quiet menace.

At her apartment, Destiny twirled in front of her mirror as her assistant zipped her into the burgundy cocktail dress. The intricate beadwork caught the light, creating a dazzling effect.

"It's perfect," Destiny said with a smile, her excitement barely contained.

Her assistant handed her a matching pair of heels. "You'll turn every head tonight."

Destiny glanced at the clock. "Let's hope one head in particular notices," she said with a playful grin, thinking of Mob-Lee.

At the Mitchell Estate, the family gathered in the grand foyer, each member a vision of 1920s glamour. Aunt Camille's floor-length gown sparkled with silver beading, her presence commanding as always. Aura-Lee's champagne-colored dress was offset by her bold crimson lips, her hair styled in flawless finger waves.

Mob-Lee emerged last, his burgundy suit tailored to perfection, a gold pocket watch gleaming against the deep fabric. The lion's head ring on his finger twinkled, a subtle but powerful symbol of his inheritance.

"You clean up well, bro," Aura-Lee teased, looping her arm through his.

"Only because you keep setting the standard," Mob-Lee shot back with a grin.

The family piled into their convoy of sleek SUVs, their arrival already a spectacle in the making.

From the balcony of the DoubleTree Hotel, Tasha watched the river flow gently by as the sky darkened. She took a long sip of her champagne, steeling herself for the night ahead.

"Do I have to attend this bullshit event?" Brandon called from the bathroom, irritation evident in his voice.

Tasha smirked, her tone smooth as silk. "Are you my man?"

"Yes!" Brandon replied, exasperated.

"Then same answer," she said simply, turning back to the view.

As she stepped inside to prepare, her thoughts drifted to Mob-Lee. The idea of facing him sent a shiver down her spine—not of fear, but of uncertainty.

Brandon emerged from the bathroom, tugging at his tie. He picked up his phone and dialed his head of security. "Keep things tight tonight," he instructed. "We never know what they might have up their sleeves."

Hanging up, Brandon's thoughts flickered to the three men he'd lost to Mob-Lee's fury after the gala. He clenched his jaw. Tonight, he'd be ready.

All over town, the streets were alive with anticipation. Cars filled with finely dressed guests headed toward the Global Strategies headquarters, their headlights cutting through the night.

The city held its breath, knowing that tonight's celebration wasn't just about a merger—it was about power, legacy, and the unspoken battles simmering beneath the surface.

As the Mitchell convoy pulled up to the entrance, Mob-Lee stepped out, his lion's ring catching the light. He glanced at Aura-Lee, a shared understanding passing between them.

"Let's make it unforgettable," he said.

Aura-Lee smiled. "Oh, we will."

The night was just beginning.

The top floor of the Global Strategies building was a glittering scene of wealth and power. Crystal chandeliers cast a golden glow over the impeccably dressed guests as the jazz band played softly in the background. Conversations buzzed with anticipation, all eyes subtly scanning the room for the night's central figures.

When the elevator doors slid open, the Mitchell family stepped out in full force, their 1920s attire a striking display of unity and style. At their center, Aura-Lee radiated confidence, her champagne dress shimmering as she raised a hand to quiet the sudden cheers.

"Sorry to disappoint, It's just me" she teased with a laugh, her voice carrying through the crowd.

The room joined in the laughter, and the Mitchells seamlessly melted into the gathering, charming their way through introductions and small talk.

Meanwhile, downstairs, Mob-Lee stood near the entrance, his lion's head ring gleaming under the soft lighting. He adjusted his cufflinks, his sharp burgundy suit a perfect blend of modern elegance and vintage flair. At 8:59 PM, his eyes flicked to his watch, a smirk curling on his lips.

"Punctual as always," he muttered to himself as three black SUVs approached.

The first car stopped, and the door swung open to reveal Booker Brown, a seasoned businessman and one of Mob-Lee's father's closest allies. Booker stepped out, his broad frame commanding respect as he shook Mob-Lee's hand firmly.

"Your parents would be so proud of you," Booker said with a warm smile before heading inside.

The second SUV rolled up, and Mob-Lee's smile vanished.

The door opened, and out stepped Tasha, her icy beauty heightened by a shimmering black gown. Following closely behind was Brandon Corvin, his sharp tuxedo matched by his sharp gaze.

Mob-Lee's jaw tightened, but he remained composed. Tasha met his eyes for a fleeting moment, her expression longing. Brandon, however, couldn't resist letting his glare linger, his unspoken challenge clear.

Neither man said a word. Tasha's heels clicked against the pavement as she and Brandon swept past Mob-Lee and into the building. The tension hung heavy in the air, but Mob-Lee let it roll off him.

The third SUV pulled up, and Mob-Lee's heart raced in anticipation. The door opened, and there she was—Destiny Knight.

Her burgundy cocktail dress was a perfect complement to his suit, its intricate beadwork catching the light with every step she took. Her presence was magnetic, her smile warm and genuine.

Mob-Lee felt his breath catch for a moment. "You look... perfect," he said, his voice softer than usual.

Destiny's eyes sparkled as she reached out to straighten his tie. "And you clean up well, Mr. Mitchell," she teased.

They shared a brief embrace, their chemistry definite, before heading into the building arm in arm.

Inside the building, Booker Brown found himself in the elevator with Brandon Corvin. The confined space only heightened the tension between them. Booker's hands clenched into fists, his mind racing with thoughts of confronting Brandon about his many transgressions.

Brandon, sensing the storm brewing, stood stiffly, refusing to make eye contact. The air was thick with unspoken animosity, and when the elevator doors finally opened, Booker practically stormed out, his presence sending a ripple of murmurs through the crowd.

The tension wasn't lost on anyone. The feud between Booker and Brandon was well-known in the business community, and their icy exchange only added to the evening's intrigue.

As the crowd settled, Tasha, ever the socialite, took the opportunity to speak up. "The guests of honor were right behind us," she announced, her voice smooth and commanding.

Just as she finished speaking, the elevator doors opened once more. Mob-Lee and Destiny stepped out together, their entrance a perfect blend of elegance and authority. The room erupted in applause and cheers, the energy shifting instantly.

Mob-Lee scanned the crowd, his lion's head ring glinting as he raised a hand in acknowledgment. Destiny, poised and radiant, held onto his arm, her presence amplifying his commanding aura.

The celebration had officially begun, and as Mob-Lee and Destiny moved through the crowd, they couldn't help but feel the weight of the night's importance. Tonight wasn't just about a merger—it was about legacy, power, and the future they were about to shape.

The jazz band transitioned into an upbeat swing number, the guests toasting and mingling as the evening unfolded. Somewhere in the crowd, rivalries simmered, alliances formed, and secrets waited to be revealed.

For Mob-Lee Mitchell, this was just the beginning.

The official merger ceremony was a grand yet efficient affair. The stage, adorned with sleek black and gold decor, gleamed under the spotlight as Destiny Knight took the podium. Her speech, polished and inspiring, painted a vision of unity and progress. She ended with a confident smile and a raised glass, her words reverberating through the crowd:

"To a future built on trust, innovation, and resilience—may this merger be a beacon for us all."

Mob-Lee followed with his usual charm, keeping the crowd captivated with a mix of humor and sentiment. "First off, I'd like to say if I seem a little too happy, it's because I might still be drunk from earlier," he quipped, earning a wave of laughter. Then his tone shifted to pride.

"This merger isn't just business—it's family. And I have to give special thanks to my twin sister, Aura-Lee, who's stepping into the role of COO. She's my rock and my compass."

Thunderous applause followed as Mob-Lee signed a document alongside Destiny, symbolically sealing the merger. Toasts were made, glasses clinked, and the band resumed, signaling the start of the evening's festivities.

The celebration was in full swing an hour later, the music loud and the drinks flowing freely. Booker Brown found Camille Mitchell by the bar, her regal presence making her easy to spot in the lively crowd.

"Camille," Booker said, extending his hand, "care to dance?"

Camille's eyebrows arched in mild surprise, but a small smile graced her lips. "Why not?" she said, setting her glass down and taking his hand.

On the dance floor, Booker's eyes never left hers as they moved to the slow rhythm. "You've still got it," he said, his tone warm but tinged with something deeper.

"You always were a charmer, Booker," Camille replied with a smirk.

Their conversation drifted to memories of old times—shared ambitions, fleeting moments of connection, and missed opportunities. Booker, emboldened by nostalgia and the evening's warmth, leaned in slightly. "I'll always wonder what could've been, Camille."

Camille held his gaze for a moment before responding with a quiet laugh. "And I'll always wonder how different our paths might've been."

Across the room, Diane Sterling fumed quietly. Her expensive silver gown shimmered as she shifted restlessly, glaring at the crowd. No one had approached her, not for conversation or acknowledgment. It was clear to her that Mob-Lee was monopolizing the evening's attention.

"Typical" she muttered under her breath, her resentment festering.

Nearby, Stanley White's patience wore thin. He had been trying to speak to Mob-Lee all night but was consistently interrupted by well-wishers and celebratory chaos. When he finally got a chance, shaking Mob-Lee's hand firmly, the moment was snatched away as Juvenile's "Back That Azz Up" blasted through the speakers.

Destiny, laughing, grabbed Mob-Lee's hand and led him to the dance floor. He grinned, mouthing a quick apology to Stanley before disappearing into the crowd to join Destiny.

Stanley's jaw tightened, his face darkening as he watched Mob-Lee and Destiny lose themselves in the music, their chemistry gyrating the the same as their bodies. His anger simmered, a boiling pot barely kept from spilling over.

At the edge of the room, Tasha Sinclair stood with her drink, her eyes locked on Mob-Lee and Destiny. Her fingers clenched the glass as jealousy flared.

Meanwhile, Brandon Corvin, determined to stir trouble, approached Robert Xavier and Vance Cruz near the bar. His voice was low but laced with hostility. "So this is how you spin your failure? Riding the coattails of Mob-Lee Mitchell?"

Robert's eyes narrowed, his expression hardening. "Careful, Corvin. Your mouth is writing checks you can't cash."

Before Brandon could escalate, Booker Brown stepped in. "That's enough," Booker said, his voice sharp and authoritative.

But before the tension could dissipate, the former Black Sky Group board members converged on Robert and Vance, their faces dark with anger.

"You ruined us!" one man hissed.
"Our livelihoods!" another spat, pointing an accusing finger.

The argument quickly drew attention, and the crowd parted slightly, giving the confrontation a visible stage. Robert and Vance stood their ground, but it was clear they were outnumbered.

"Everyone calm down," Booker urged, stepping between the groups. But the animosity was thick, threatening to boil over at any moment.

As the night wore on, the celebration began to wind down. Guests offered their congratulations and farewells, filtering out of the building with smiles and lingering excitement.

Destiny shared a quiet moment with Isabel Hunter, her foster mother, who had arrived late in the evening.

"I'm proud of you, Destiny," Isabel said, her voice soft but sincere. "You've come so far."

Destiny smiled, hugging Isabel tightly. "I wouldn't be here without you," she said, her voice barely above a whisper.

Downstairs, however, the night was far from over for Robert and Vance. The heated argument from earlier had only grown worse, with more disgruntled individuals joining the fray.

"You're nothing but cowards hiding behind your money," one man snarled.

"Say that again," Vance growled, stepping forward.

The tension snapped like a taut wire as the argument turned physical, shoves being exchanged as security scrambled to intervene.

Unbeknownst to them, in the shadows of the parking garage, a group of unidentified figures lingered, their presence ominous. Their eyes followed Robert and Vance as the fight spilled into the open.

One man in the group spoke quietly into a phone. "They're still here. Proceed as planned."

The stage was set for a confrontation that would shake the night's fragile peace.

The sound of four sharp gunshots tore through the tense confrontation outside the Global

Strategies building, sending the crowd into a frenzy. Guests and staff scattered, ducking behind vehicles or rushing into waiting cars Tires screeched as some fled the scene without hesitation.

Vance Cruz collapsed to the ground, blood seeping through his suit from two gunshot wounds. He lay motionless, his chest barely rising and falling as a pool of crimson spread beneath him. Panic engulfed the scene

Before anyone could process the chaos, a black van screeched to a halt nearby. Its back doors flew open, and masked figures jumped out, grabbing Robert Xavier with precision and force. Despite his struggles, they overpowered him, shoving him into the van before speeding off into the night.

The last guests leaving the party arrived at a chilling scene: blood on the pavement, police tape cordoning off the area, and evidence markers scattered around. Red and blue lights bathed the scene in an eerie glow, accompanied by the wail of sirens. Officers secured the perimeter as paramedics worked swiftly to stabilize Vance and load him into an ambulance.

Inside the building, Mob-Lee remained oblivious to the unfolding chaos. He was sharing a final drink with Destiny when his security detail rushed in, speaking in hurried tones.

"We need to get Ms. Knight to her car immediately," one of them said.

Mob-Lee frowned. "What's going on?"

'There's been an incident outside," the man replied grimly.

Without hesitation, Mob-Lee signaled Destiny to follow. As she was ushered into her waiting SUV, Mob-Lee turned to one of his guards "Stay with her until she's home safe. Don't leave her side."

Destiny, sensing the gravity of his tone, nodded, though concern flickered in her eyes. "Be careful, Mob-Lee."

Mob-Lee stepped outside to find chaos contained within the flashing lights and organized chaos of a crime scene. Officers controlled the scene as investigators examined the area with meticulous focus.

Detective Aiden Finn approached Mob-Lee. His sharp features and piercing blue eyes reflected both determination and weariness. He wasted no time.

"I take it you didn't see anything either," Finn said, his thick Irish accent cutting through the noise.

Mob-Lee crossed his arms. "I don't even know what happened. What's going on out here?"

Finn sighed. "Four shots fired. One man hit- he's alive but in critical condition. EMTs just took him to the hospital. And.." He paused for emphasis. "There's an alleged kidnapping Several witnesses claim they saw a man forced into a black van that fled the scene."

Mob-Lee's stomach sank, dread pooling in his chest. "This is my company's building. I'll help however I can.

Finn handed him a card. "I'll be in touch. And if you think of anything, call me."

After clearing Mob-Lee to leave, Finn turned his attention back to the scene.

As Mob-Lee climbed into the back seat of his SUV, his mind raced. Who was shot? Who was taken? And why? The pieces didn't fit, but the dark web of enemies surrounding his family seemed to tighten.

The vibration of his phone in his pocket snapped him out of his thoughts. He pulled it out to see a flurry of notifications

Aura-Lee: "Are you okay? Please call me ASAP!"

Aunt Camille: "Call me. It's urgent!"

Before he could dial, the screen flickered and went black. Dead battery. Mob-Lee cursed under his breath, frustration building.

'Step on it," he barked at the driver. "I need to get back to the estate now.

The vehicle sped through the dark streets, the city lights blurring past as Mob-Lee tried to calm the storm inside him. Answers were waiting at the Mitchell Estate, but so were more questions.

Tension mounts as the crime scene deepens the mystery. Mob-Lee finds himself at the center of a storm with enemies striking from the shadows. The stakes are higher than ever, and the Mitchell family's safety-and their legacy-hangs in the balance.

Chapter 6: Storm brewing

The Mitchell Estate stood solemn under the pale glow of the moon. Mob-Lee's SUV pulled into the extended driveway, the flashing lights of a single patrol car illuminating the grand entrance. His stomach twisted as he stepped out, the scene before him sharp and disconcerting.

Aunt Camille sat on the mansion's steps, sobbing into Aura-Lee's shoulder. Logan stood rigid a few feet away, locked in conversation with a police officer.

As Mob-Lee approached, Officer Mike Furman turned to him, squinting. "Is this the missing one? He matches the description you gave me."

Logan's voice shot out like a bullet. "No. Just because he's Black, you assume he matches? That's the problem with—"

Furman held up a hand, his posture stiffening as his fingers brushed his holster. "No need to act all wild," he said defensively. "I was just asking."

The tension was engulfing everyone, the air thick with unspoken words. Furman tipped his hat and concluded, "We'll be in touch with any updates." He got into his patrol car, the strobing lights dimming as he drove off into the night.

Mob-Lee walked toward his family, his voice measured but urgent. "What's going on?"

Logan's shoulders sagged as he ran a hand over his head. "It's bad, Mob-Lee. Vance was shot—twice. He's in surgery now." Logan hesitated, the next words heavy. "And Robert… Robert's missing. Kidnapped."

Mob-Lee's heart sank as his aunt looked up at him, her tear-streaked face etched with despair. "One son fighting for his life, and the other… God knows where," Camille whispered before breaking into fresh sobs.

Mob-Lee wrapped his arms around her, his voice soft but firm. "We'll get through this, Cam. We'll find Robert, and Vance will pull through."

She clung to him for a moment before stepping back, wiping her eyes. "I need to be at the hospital," she said, turning to Logan. "Let's go."

Logan nodded, and together they headed for the car.

Inside the estate, the air was tense and heavy. Mob-Lee dropped into a chair in the expansive living room while Aura-Lee paced, her arms crossed tightly across her chest.

"Who could've done this?" she muttered, her sharp heels clicking against the marble floor. "There were so many people angry with Robert and Vance. Brandon Corvin, the Black Sky Group board members…"

Mob-Lee rubbed his temples, thinking back to the party. "Brandon's a coward. He wouldn't do it himself, but he might've hired someone. And the Black Sky board? They've got every reason to want revenge after what Robert and Vance pulled at the gala."

Aura-Lee stopped pacing, her eyes narrowing. "So we're surrounded by suspects."

"Feels like it."

As Mob-Lee shrugged off his suit jacket, an envelope slipped from the inner pocket, thudding onto the floor. He stared at it for a beat before picking it up.

"You didn't read yours yet, did you?" he asked, looking at Aura-Lee.

She shook her head, her brow furrowed. "No. Should I?"

"Go get it. Let's see what they have to say."

Aura-Lee disappeared down a hallway, returning moments later with an envelope in hand. The siblings sat side by side, the room silent as they opened the letters.

Mob-Lee read his aloud first. "Welcome back. Stay safe, because enemies are everywhere. Protect the family." His jaw clenched. "Straight to the point."

Aura-Lee's eyes darted across the page. "Tell Mob-Lee everything we told you about everyone. Stay safe. Be your brother's eyes and ears."

She looked up, her face pale. "What does that even mean?"

Mob-Lee folded his letter carefully, sliding it into his pocket. "It means they knew this was coming. At least some of it."

Later, as the house settled into an uneasy quiet, Mob-Lee pulled out his phone and dialed Destiny. She picked up almost immediately.

"Mob-Lee," she said, her voice laced with worry. "Are you okay? I heard about the shooting."

"I'm fine," he assured her. "But things are… complicated. Are you safe?"

"Yes, I'm fine," she said. "Just worried about you. Let's skip the meeting tomorrow?"

"Just give me a day and then we'll meet," he said firmly. "We'll talk more then."

"Good. Just… be careful, okay?"

"I will."

Across town, Diane Sterling stood on the balcony of her beachfront mansion, the waves crashing against the shore below. A glass of wine dangled from her fingers as she stared into the night.

Behind her, Edgar stood silently in the doorway, his expression unreadable.

"It's done," Diane said into her phone. "The dossier has been sent to the FBI. With this information, we can bring that arrogant fool to his knees."

She ended the call and turned to Edgar, a smile playing on her lips. "We'll see how long that boy stays on top."

Edgar nodded silently, his loyalty unwavering as Diane turned back to the ocean, the wheels of her scheme spinning faster with each passing moment.

The sterile beeps of the heart monitor echoed in the dimly lit hospital room. Vance lay motionless, his face drained, his body weak from the trauma he had endured. Camille Mitchell sat beside him, clutching his hand with both of hers, her thumb brushing gently against his knuckles. The faint glow of the machines reflected in her tear-filled eyes.

One bullet wound had ripped through his shoulder, and another had narrowly missed his heart. The surgeon had said it was a miracle he survived, but Camille found no solace in miracles. This wasn't fate; this was someone's doing. And they would pay.

"You fight, Vance," Camille whispered, her voice trembling. "You hear me? You fight. Because I swear on everything I have, whoever did this to you will answer to me. Every last one of them."

The door opened, and Logan entered with two steaming cups of coffee. He handed one to Camille and sat down in the chair opposite her.

"How's he doing?" Logan asked, his voice quiet but tense.

"He's stable," Camille replied, her voice steadying as she took the coffee. "But no updates. No answers. Nothing."

Logan exhaled heavily, leaning back in his chair. "Answers are coming. Whoever thought they could come after the family is in for a rude awakening."

Before Camille could respond, there was a sharp knock at the door. Officer Mike Furman stepped in, his uniform crisp but his demeanor anything but professional.

"I need to speak to Mr. Cruz," Furman said, holding a small notepad.

Logan stood immediately. "He's unconscious. You'll have to come back later."

Furman smirked and ignored Logan, turning to Camille. "Ms. Mitchell, do you think this could be gang-related? Or maybe drugs? A lot of shootings like this usually are."

Camille's eyes darkened, and she stood, her imposing presence filling the room. "Are you accusing my son of being involved with gangs or drugs, Officer Furman?"

Furman shrugged. "Just exploring the possibilities. Just because you've got a shiny title doesn't mean—"

"Doesn't mean what?" Camille snapped, her voice rising. "I am a Supreme Court Justice, and I will not tolerate baseless accusations against my family. My son is fighting for his life in this bed, and you dare come here with your disrespectful insinuations?"

Logan stepped closer, his voice low and dangerous. "You heard her. Get out. Now."

Furman's hand drifted toward his notepad. "Fine," he muttered, scribbling something down. "I'll be back when he wakes up."

He turned on his heel and left the room, his boots echoing down the hall. Logan let out a slow breath and glanced at Camille.

"Let's focus on Vance. That idiot isn't worth the energy," he said.

Back at the Mitchell Estate, the butler opened the grand doors to find a courier holding a plain white envelope. The butler accepted the package with a polite nod and walked it directly to Mob-Lee, who was in his study.

Mob-Lee sat at the desk, the envelope in his hands. Robert's name was scrawled on the front in thick, jagged letters. He tore it open, his stomach twisting with unease. Inside was a single sheet of paper with a chilling message:

"$10 million in 48 hours, or Robert will be sent back to you in pieces."

Mob-Lee's grip tightened on the paper, his mind racing. He grabbed his phone and sent a group text to Logan, Aunt Camille, and Aura-Lee.

Mob-Lee: They want a ransom. $10 million. We have 48 hours.

Logan read the message and frowned. "I need to be out there helping find him," he said to Camille, standing in the hospital room. "I'll follow up on some leads. I'll call if I find anything."

Camille nodded, her eyes still fixed on Vance. "Be careful, Logan. And bring him home."

Back at the estate, Logan delved into Robert and Vance's activities over the past month, combing through their schedules, texts, and emails. Patterns began to emerge—secretive meetings, cryptic notes, and locations that seemed too familiar. Each meeting seemed tied to one thing: the impending merger.

"Who the hell were you meeting?" Logan muttered to himself, jotting down notes. He grabbed his coat and car keys, determined to trace Robert's steps.

The next morning, Mob-Lee arrived at Optimized Education headquarters. Destiny was already waiting in her office, a folder of documents spread across her desk. She looked up as he entered, her face brightening.

"Hey," she said. "You look tired."

Mob-Lee sighed, dropping into the chair opposite her. "Tired doesn't even begin to cover it."

Destiny leaned forward, concern etched on her face. "Any news on Robert or Vance?"

"Vance is stable. Robert…" Mob-Lee hesitated, running a hand through his hair. "There's a ransom demand. Ten million dollars, 48 hours."

Destiny's eyes widened. "Oh my God. What are you going to do?"

"Figure out who's behind this and end it," Mob-Lee said firmly. "But it's not just them I'm worried about. This shooting—it could destroy the merger. The board will panic. Investors will pull out. We could lose everything."

Destiny reached across the desk, resting her hand on his. "We've worked too hard to let that happen. The merger will survive this. And so will you."

Mob-Lee managed a small smile. "I hope you're right. Just… keep your eyes open. If anything feels off while you're reviewing the documents, let me know immediately."

"I will," Destiny promised.

They scheduled a meeting for the next day with the Optimized Education board and the Vice President of Operations from Global Strategies—Tasha Sinclair to formally sign all documents.

Back in Miami, Brandon Corvin leaned back in his leather chair, his feet propped on his glass desk. He ended his phone call with a satisfied grin, tossing his phone onto the desk.

"It's all coming together," he said to himself, swirling a glass of bourbon. "The Mitchells won't know what hit them."

He raised his glass to the skyline outside his window, a wicked smile playing on his lips.

Logan sat in the quiet of the Mitchell estate's study, surrounded by Robert and Vance's schedules, financial reports, and location data. His laptop hummed faintly as he scrolled through the details. Most of their activities appeared mundane—luncheons, board meetings, and social outings—but two entries from their schedules stopped him cold:

R.X. and K.M. - Smyrna - 10 PM, September 10th

Cruz and Dubois - Eureka - 12 AM, September 11th

Logan frowned and leaned back in his chair, the names and places ringing bells he couldn't yet place. He tapped his pen against his temple. "Smyrna. Eureka. What the hell were they doing there?"

He pulled up geolocation data from Robert and Vance's phones. Both had pinged at those exact locations during the times noted. These weren't coincidences; they were deliberate moves.

"Smyrna," Logan murmured to himself. His stomach twisted. "The Bottom."

The Northside district was notorious for its underground gambling dens, extortion rackets, and gang activity. It was enemy territory.

And Eureka—Logan didn't need to dig to know the significance.

"Eureka Gardens," he muttered, the name alone conjuring a flood of memories.

Logan stood and paced the room, his mind drifting back to the days when he and Deacon Mitchell had run the streets of Jacksonville. Smyrna, "The Bottom," had always been a place where alliances were tested and violence loomed. Enemy territory.

But Eureka Gardens, known as "The Bricks," was worse. The sprawling apartment complex had been a battlefield until Deacon had brokered a truce between his Coastline Mafia and the Eureka Gangsters. The truce had allowed Deacon to dominate the city, but it was always fragile.

Logan rubbed his temples as flashbacks struck like lightning—Deacon standing tall amidst a hail of bullets, commanding respect through sheer willpower. Those days were behind them, but the shadows they cast were long.

"These places aren't just random stops," Logan muttered, returning to his desk. "They're messages."

Logan dove back into the data. Smyrna and Eureka weren't the only anomalies. Over the past few months, Robert and Vance had attended a string of secretive meetings, most of them late at night in obscure locations. Logan highlighted the two most recent entries:

Robert (R.X.): Smyrna, 10 PM

Vance (Cruz): Eureka, 12 AM

"They split up," Logan realized. "Why would they do that?"

He checked their bank accounts, looking for any unusual activity. Nothing concrete. Then he examined their call logs. A string of unlisted numbers and brief conversations stood out, all clustered around the dates of the meetings.

"What were you two into?" Logan growled, his frustration mounting.

His phone buzzed—a text from Camille.

Camille: Any progress?

Logan hesitated before replying.

Logan: I think Furman might be right about something. Robert and Vance were deep into something dangerous. Smyrna and Eureka are key.

The response felt like a betrayal of his gut instinct, but the evidence was piling up. If Furman's hunch about gang or criminal ties was true, Robert and Vance might have been dealing with forces far beyond their control.

Another message came in, this time from Mob-Lee:

Mob-Lee: Anything I should know?

Logan typed back:

Logan: Not yet. I'll update you soon.

Logan stared at the map of Jacksonville spread out on the desk. He marked Smyrna and Eureka, noting the times and connections. The pieces were falling into place, but the picture they painted was grim.

His phone buzzed again. This time, it was Camille calling.

"Logan," she said, her voice heavy with tension. "Do you have a lead?"

"I think so," Logan replied. "But you're not going to like it. Smyrna and Eureka... they're not just locations. They're warnings. Robert and Vance were playing with fire, and now it's catching up to us."

"Do what you need to," Camille said firmly. "Find out who's behind this."

Logan nodded, though she couldn't see him. "I'm heading out now. I'll keep you posted."

He grabbed his jacket and a concealed firearm before heading for the door. The streets of Smyrna and Eureka weren't just memories anymore—they were battlefields he had to navigate once again.

Camille sat curled under the warmth of a cashmere blanket in the corner of Vance's hospital room. The beeps and faint whirs of machines filled the silence. Her gaze lingered on Vance's still form, his face pale but calm, and a wave of memories began to stir.

Her eyelids fluttered shut as she drifted back to that fateful day years ago, the day she became a mother.

The fluorescent lights of the delivery room felt blinding as Camille clenched her fists, her body wracked with pain. Twelve hours—twelve excruciating hours of labor. She remembered Juan's voice, calm yet filled with tension, trying to encourage her.

"You've got this, Camille. Just one more push," he had said, gripping her hand.

Her mind flashed further back, to the days leading up to this moment. The doctor had confidently declared, "It's a boy." Camille had felt a rush of emotions—joy, relief, and a surge of determination. She'd vowed to give her child every opportunity her family's name could offer.

But naming him had been another battle entirely.

She could still picture Juan pacing the nursery, throwing out suggestions.

"Vance," he said, smiling. "It's strong, unique."

Camille had countered with her own ideas, torn between two options.

"Robert," she suggested, the name a tribute to her grandfather, a brilliant but unyielding man who had shaped the Mitchell legacy. "Or maybe Xavier. It has a regal sound, don't you think?"

They had debated for hours, never truly settling on a decision.

Her memory shifted to the delivery room again. She could feel the intense relief as she pushed her son into the world, his cries filling the room.

"A boy," the doctor announced as Juan kissed her forehead.

The baby weighed 9 pounds, 15 ounces, a healthy, squirming bundle. Camille watched as Juan cut the umbilical cord and held him for the first time.

"Vance," Juan said softly, his voice filled with pride.

But then, the room erupted into chaos.

"There's another one," the doctor said, his voice urgent yet controlled.

Camille's heart stopped. Another baby?

Juan's voice cut through the haze. "A second baby?"

Minutes later, she heard the wail of her second child. Exhausted but exhilarated, she felt the weight of the world shift onto her shoulders.

"Robert or Xavier?" Juan had asked, cradling the tiny infant.

Her heart had spoken for her. "Robert Xavier," she whispered, her decision firm.

Juan smiled. "My boys, Vance Cruz and Robert Xavier Cruz."

But Camille felt a pang of unease. She loved Juan, but the Cruz name belonged to his lineage, his story. Her legacy mattered too.

"No," she said softly but with conviction. "Robert Xavier will be a Mitchell. I want to contribute to my family's legacy as well."

Juan had paused, looking at her with a mix of surprise and understanding. He nodded. "Robert Xavier Mitchell, then."

It was a choice that had defined their family's future.

Camille's eyes opened as she stared at Vance's unmoving form. Her heart ached at the memory of those early days, the hope and promise they had held. Her voice broke the silence, soft but resolute.

"Wake up, Vance," she murmured, reaching out to hold his hand. "Wake up so we can find your brother."

For a moment, there was no response. Then, slowly, Vance's eyes fluttered open, his gaze hazy but alive.

"Mom?" he croaked weakly, his voice barely audible.

Camille exhaled, tears streaming down her face as she leaned closer. "I'm here, sweetheart. You're safe."

But the fire in her voice returned as she added, "And we're going to get Robert back. I promise you."

Vance's lips twitched in the faintest hint of a smile, and Camille's resolve only hardened.

Aura-Lee sat in the back seat of her chauffeured G-Wagon, gripping the leather armrest as the city lights blurred past the tinted windows. Her thoughts raced faster than the vehicle, replaying memories of Robert Xavier and Vance.

Her polished demeanor cracked as she leaned her head against the cool glass, letting her mind drift back two years ago to their 25th birthday party.

The East Wing balcony of the Mitchell Estate overlooked the sprawling grounds, bathed in golden light from the ongoing celebration inside. Aura-Lee stood between her cousins, Robert and Vance, each with a glass of bourbon in hand. The scent of cigars and expensive cologne hung in the air.

Robert leaned against the railing, swaying slightly. "Aura, you're the smartest and most reliable person in the family. We need you to hold onto something for us."

Vance chimed in, his grin mischievous. "We mean it, Aura-Lee. You're the only person we trust."

Aura-Lee raised a skeptical brow. "What is it?"

Robert pulled a small, silver key from his pocket and pressed it into her hand.

"A locker key," Vance explained, his voice slurred but steady enough to convey importance.

Aura-Lee studied the key. "Why am I holding this? What's in the locker?"

They exchanged a glance, then said in unison, "Rainy day fund." They burst into laughter, clinking their glasses.

Vance straightened, elaborating through his chuckles. "We've been putting away two million a year since we turned 15. That locker's got 10 million in it."

Aura-Lee's eyes widened. "Ten million? For what?"

Robert shrugged, his expression suddenly serious. "You know... shit happens."

The memory faded as Aura-Lee tightened her grip on the key in her hand. Now, two years later, she was racing to that locker, praying it wasn't an empty promise made under drunken bravado.

The G-Wagon pulled up to an unassuming storage facility in the industrial district. Her driver, Cedric, stepped out to open her door, followed closely by her personal guard, Samuel.

"This is it," Aura-Lee said, her voice steady but tense. She entered the facility and followed the numbered corridors until she reached the unit matching the key.

Her heart pounded as she inserted the key and turned it. Instead of a small locker, the door opened to a walk-in closet-sized space filled with black duffel bags.

Aura-Lee let out a shaky breath, gesturing to Cedric and Samuel. "Load them up. Quickly."

As they hauled the bags to the car, Aura-Lee unzipped one. Stacks of hundred-dollar bills stared back at her. She began counting.

"Two million per bag," she muttered, her voice a mix of disbelief and relief. Seven bags. That's 14 million.

Her brow furrowed. "They lied," she murmured, a faint smile playing on her lips. "But in the best way."

She closed the last bag, her mind piecing it together. "They must've had their own keys. This was just the backup. Smart."

The G-Wagon rolled to a stop at the Mitchell Estate. Aura-Lee wasted no time responding to the group text.

Aura-Lee: I have the money.

Moments later, her phone vibrated with Mob-Lee's reply.

Mob-Lee: Where the fuck did you get it?

Aura-Lee: I'll explain later.

Logan's response came next, a simple pair of praying hands.

Aura-Lee stepped into the grand foyer with her guard in tow, each carrying a duffel bag. She found Mob-Lee in the study, pacing with the ransom note in hand.

"Any word yet?" she asked urgently. "Address? Time? Location? Phone number? Anything?"

Mob-Lee shook his head and handed her the note.

"Nothing yet. Just this," he said, frustration lacing his voice.

Aura-Lee scanned the note again, the demand clear: 10 million within 48 hours or Robert will be sent home in pieces.

She looked up at her brother with determination. "It's been 16 hours. We still have time. They'll reach out, and we're ready."

Mob-Lee's shoulders relaxed ever so slightly. "Let's hope so," he muttered.

Their phones buzzed simultaneously. Camille's name lit up the screen.

Camille: Vance is awake!

Aura-Lee and Mob-Lee let out a collective sigh of relief.

"Finally, some good news," Aura-Lee said, a small smile breaking through her worry.

Mob-Lee nodded. "We needed this."

For a brief moment, the tension in the room eased. It seemed as though the pieces were falling into place.

As the clock ticked forward, the estate settled into an uneasy quiet. Aura-Lee double-checked the money, counting and recounting to ensure nothing was missing. Mob-Lee poured over the ransom note, searching for hidden clues.

But deep in the shadows, trouble brewed. A blacked-out Jeep parked a mile away from the estate, its windows rolled down just enough for a cigarette to glow faintly in the night.

Inside, a man ended a call, his wicked smile illuminated by the ember.

Back at the estate, the faint feeling of relief that had taken hold of the Mitchell family would soon be shattered. The storm was coming.

Chapter 7

The Mitchell Estate was unusually quiet, the tension palpable as everyone awaited the next move. Logan Livingston sat alone in the estate's armory, cleaning his Glock with methodical precision. His mind was elsewhere, turning over every detail of the last 24 hours. Robert's kidnapping. Vance's shooting. None of it sat right.

"This ain't random," he muttered to himself, gripping the gun tighter.

Convinced the answers lay in the streets, Logan pulled out his phone and dialed a number he hadn't called in years.

The gruff voice on the other end answered after the first ring. "What's good?"

Logan exhaled. "I need a favor, Deuce."

The old boat dock off Broward Road looked the same as it did decades ago, a relic of their past lives. Logan parked his black Range Rover and stepped out, the cool night air filled with the sound of lapping water.

Deuce was already there, leaning against the hood of a Cadillac Escalade, a cigar dangling from his lips. He was older now, graying at the temples, but still carried the same commanding presence.

"Long time, no see, no hear, no nothing, Dutchie," Deuce greeted, his voice a blend of bitterness and nostalgia.

Logan stepped forward, clasping Deuce's hand in their old gang handshake, a series of intricate movements perfected over years.

"At least you remember the shake," Deuce said with a smirk, puffing on his cigar.

Logan didn't waste time. "What did you find out?"

Deuce's expression turned serious. "The courier was hired by the boys from the bottom, so you already know they're tied to that. But the where..." He shrugged. "That's a different story. Nobody's seen or heard anything. And you know the streets talk, especially for a price."

Logan nodded, his jaw tight. "And the shooting?"

Deuce scratched his beard. "Don't seem connected. But I did hear one of them youngins say they was 'smoking on that Vance' the other day. Didn't think much of it until now. Did old boy die?"

Logan's voice was firm. "No."

The two men locked eyes, the weight of their shared history unspoken but heavy. Logan handed Deuce two large envelopes.

"It's all there," Logan said.

Deuce grinned, tucking the envelopes under his arm. "Dutchie never comes up short. I know." He paused, flicking ash from his cigar. "Oh yeah, that youngin was from out Eureka. Might be worth a look."

Logan gave a curt nod. "preciate it."

They shook hands again, and Logan turned to leave.

As Logan drove away, his mind raced. "Eureka," he repeated under his breath. The name triggered memories of past turf wars, alliances, and betrayals.

He gripped the steering wheel tighter, the pieces of the puzzle beginning to fit together. The courier was from "the bottom," but

Vance's shooting seemed like a separate issue—someone trying to make a name for himself?

Logan pressed a button on his dashboard, activating his secure line. "Mob-Lee, you there?"

Mob-Lee's voice crackled through the speakers. "What's up?"

"I'm heading into enemy territory. Boys from the bottom might've grabbed Robert. Vance's shooting could be unrelated, but I'm not ruling anything out."

Mob-Lee's tone shifted. "You need backup?"

"Nah," Logan replied. "Not yet. Just keep your phone close."

The atmosphere changed as Logan drove deeper into "the bottom". The streets were dimly lit, lined with graffiti-covered buildings and shadowy figures watching his car pass.

Logan slowed as he approached a rundown block known for its criminal activity. He parked, stepped out, and surveyed the area. His tailored suit and confident stride made him stand out, but his reputation preceded him.

A group of young men lounging on a stoop watched him approach, their postures tense. One of them, a wiry teenager with a scar running down his cheek, stood up.

"You lost, old man?" the teen sneered.

Logan smirked, his hand resting casually on the gun tucked into his waistband. "Nah. I'm exactly where I need to be."

The tension in the air was thick as Logan stepped closer. He wasn't just here for answers—he was here to send a message.

The storm was no longer brewing; it was about to break.

As Logan steps closer to the porch, a man about Mob-Lee's age appears from the shadows, casually rolling a blunt with practiced ease. The scent of marijuana mingles with the damp, musty air.

The man smirks, his gold teeth catching the faint light. "How can I help you, old head?"

Logan doesn't flinch. His voice is steady. "I'm looking for Big Boy."

The man's grin widens as laughter erupts from the teens lounging nearby. "Oooh, my pops, huh? Well, he ain't here, bruh. You could catch him... in the next life, when he gets out the pen."

Logan's jaw tightens. He hadn't expected this. "Who's running things now?"

The man takes a slow drag from his blunt, blowing the smoke lazily into the air. "That'd be me. Kevin Marks Junior to my elders. TopBoy to my shottas."

At his words, the teens on the porch rise to their feet, guns gleaming under the porch light. AR-15s, Glocks, and sawed-off shotguns are brandished with quiet confidence.

Logan remains calm, his hand resting lightly on the edge of his jacket. "I'm Logan Livingston," he says evenly. "I have a few questions, TopBoy, if you have the time."

TopBoy stares at him for a long moment before shrugging. "Come on in."

The group parts to let Logan through, the tension thick in the air. The trailer, worn and rusted on the outside, is a striking contrast inside. The decor is modern and luxurious: plush leather couches, a glass coffee table, and a 70-inch television mounted on the wall. A faint scent of lavender hangs in the air.

TopBoy gestures grandly toward the couch. "Mi casa es su casa."

Logan scans the room but remains standing.

Logan cuts straight to the point. "An associate of mine has gone missing. I'd like to know if you have any clue where he might be."

TopBoy leans back in his chair, studying Logan like a cat sizing up its prey. "And why would I know anything about that?"

"Because I know how this works," Logan replies, his tone sharp. "People like you always know what's moving in your territory."

TopBoy chuckles darkly, his demeanor shifting. "You got balls, old man, I'll give you that." His voice hardens. "But coming here, asking me questions like you got some authority? That's disrespectful."

The teens from the porch enter, spreading out around the room, their weapons conspicuous.

TopBoy's eyes gleam with menace. "Let me break it down for you, Dutchie. You ain't running shit around here no more. This ain't your playground. You step into my house, you better come correct, or you don't step out at all."

Logan remains silent, his heart pounding. He feels the shift in power, the weight of his vulnerability sinking in.

TopBoy stands, towering over Logan. "Now, out of respect for what you used to be, I'll let you walk outta here alive. But you don't come back unless you got something real for me. Understood?"

Logan gives a curt nod, his face a mask.

TopBoy smirks, leaning in close. "I'll be in touch... Dutchie."

The mention of his old street name sends a chill through Logan. How does this kid know him? How much else does he know?

As Logan steps outside, the humid night air feels weighted. He glances back at the trailer, now illuminated in the moonlight.

He climbs into his car, his mind racing. Who is this kid? How does he know my past? The realization sinks in: he's in deeper than he thought.

Logan checks his watch. 16 hours left. He grips the steering wheel, frustration and fear boiling inside him. His biggest lead just turned into a dead end—or worse, a trap.

The storm was far from over, and Logan knew he'd just scratched the surface of something far more dangerous than he anticipated.

Tension mounts as Logan drives away, knowing that the clock is ticking and the stakes are higher than ever.

The low hum of fluorescent lights buzzes faintly in Vance's hospital room. Camille sits rigid beside the bed, her hands folded tightly, betraying her inner turmoil. The quiet is interrupted by a sharp knock at the door.

Detective Aiden Finn enters first, his tall frame commanding attention. Officer Mike Furman follows, his expression hardened and distrustful.

"Mrs. Mitchell," Finn begins, his tone clipped but polite, "we believe we have a lead on the shooting, but we need your son's cooperation to confirm it."

Camille's sharp eyes narrow. "Ask your questions."

Furman casts her a skeptical glance, his lips twitching as if holding back a retort. Finn gestures toward Vance, who winces as he struggles to sit up straighter.

Finn pulls out a worn manila folder and withdraws a glossy photo. He places it deliberately on the table next to Vance.

"Do you recognize this man?"

Vance's gaze flickers to the image. His face tightens, and his fingers grip the blanket covering his legs. "No. Never seen him before."

Finn's lips press into a thin line as he retrieves another photo from the folder. This one hits harder—it's the same man, but he's standing shoulder-to-shoulder with Vance in a candid shot outside a dimly lit café.

"Are you sure?" Finn presses, his voice sharp enough to cut through the tense air.

Vance's breathing quickens, his eyes darting to Camille, then to the photo. "I—uh...I don't think so," he stammers, but his voice lacks conviction.

Finn steps closer, looming over the bed. "Don't lie to me, Mr. Cruz. This man might be tied to your shooting—and your brother's disappearance."

Vance groans loudly, a guttural sound that seems more an attempt to deflect than an expression of pain.

"Enough," Camille snaps, her voice slicing through the tension. She turns to her son, her tone softer but firm. "Tell them what you know. It might help bring your brother home."

Vance exhales shakily, visibly defeated. He shifts, grimacing as he props himself up against the pillows.

"Fine," he mutters. "Yes, I know him. His name is Bernard Dubois."

Finn's brow furrows. "Is he connected to the shooting?"

"I don't know," Vance says quickly, his voice tinged with panic. "I can't be sure."

Finn isn't satisfied. "What were your dealings with him?"

Vance hesitates, his mind racing. He chooses his words carefully, knowing the weight they carry. "He...wanted to invest in a business deal I was working on. The day we took that picture, I told him the deal wasn't happening anymore. That's it."

"And you think that would give him motive to try to kill you?" Finn's voice is a dangerous mix of curiosity and frustration. "If so, we can protect you—but you need to cooperate."

Before Vance can respond, Camille stands abruptly, her presence commanding the room. "That's enough. We'll speak to you another time—with our lawyers present."

Finn glances at Furman, who shakes his head subtly, his disdain clear. "Mrs. Mitchell, your son's cooperation could save lives—his own included," Finn says, his voice firm but imploring.

Camille's icy gaze doesn't waver. "The police can't protect anyone."

Vance's face is drained, his hands trembling slightly, but he remains silent.

Finn exhales sharply, gathering the photos and shoving them back into the folder. "We'll be in touch," he says curtly.

The officers leave, the door closing with a heavy thud that seems to echo in the quiet room.

The silence stretches on, thick with unspoken fears. Camille turns to Vance, her voice low and furious. "Not another word about Bernard. Let me deal with this."

Before Vance can respond, Camille's phone buzzes in her hand, the screen flashing with an unknown number. The room stills as she hesitates, her thumb hovering over the green button.

She answers on the third ring. "Hello?"

For a moment, there's only static, then a voice crackles through the line—hoarse, trembling, and unmistakable.

"Mom..." Robert's voice is faint, but the desperation is clear. "We're running out of time."

Camille shoots to her feet, her composure fracturing. "Robert? Robert! Where are you? Who has you? Hello?" Her words tumble out in a frantic rush.

The line hisses, then goes dead.

"Robert!" Camille screams, her voice raw and anguished. She stares at the phone, her hands shaking as if willing it to ring again.

The heart monitor beside Vance beeps erratically, reflecting his growing panic. Nurses peek into the room but quickly retreat when Camille waves them off.

Vance's voice is shaky. "What...what did he say?"

Camille doesn't answer immediately. She dials another number with trembling fingers, pressing the phone to her ear.

"It's me," she says when the line connects. Her voice is steadier now, but her eyes burn with urgency. "We need to move. Get the family together—now."

The storm outside mirrors the tension within. Every second feels like an eternity, the weight of Robert's cryptic call suffocating the room. With time slipping away, the Mitchells are left to face the growing darkness—and the horrifying possibility that it may already be too late.

Logan's text is short but clear: Hospital. 30 minutes.

Thirty minutes later, the Mitchell clan gathers around Vance's hospital bed. The room feels depressing, the tension suffocating as everyone awaits Camille's update.

Camille, her voice steady but tinged with urgency, addresses the group. "I received a call from Robert. It was brief, but it's clear—we're running out of time. Twelve hours left."

Logan speaks up, his expression grim. "We don't have time to trace the call. From what I've pieced together, Vance's hit was ordered out of Eureka."

Vance visibly stiffens, shifting uncomfortably in the bed. His nervousness doesn't go unnoticed.

"And," Logan continues, "the boys from the bottom are likely behind Robert's disappearance. I just don't have solid proof yet."

Aura-Lee leans in close to Vance, her voice barely audible as she whispers, "The rainy day fund is secure. You don't need to worry about that."

Vance exhales shakily, avoiding eye contact.

Mob-Lee steps forward, his jaw tight. "What can I do?"

Logan places a firm hand on his shoulder. "Keep your head down and your eyes open. You'll need both in the hours ahead."

In a dimly lit, grimy automotive garage on the outskirts of town, Robert hangs by a thick metal chain wrapped around his wrists. His feet barely touch the ground, his body battered and bloodied. Every shallow breath sends a fresh wave of pain through his chest.

Six men loiter nearby, armed but relaxed, joking about how they'll spend their share of the ransom.

"I'm buying me a jet ski," one laughs, flipping through a crumpled magazine.

Another scoffs. "Man, you can't even swim."

On a scarred wooden table sits a timer, its red numbers steadily counting down. 10 hours left.

Robert closes his swollen eyes, silently praying for deliverance.

Outside the hospital, Mob-Lee leans against a cold brick wall, his phone pressed to his ear. The line clicks, and Destiny's voice comes through, her concern evident.

"Mob-Lee, what's going on? Are you okay?"

He exhales, running a hand across his head. "It's...complicated. But it should all be over soon."

"Soon?" Her voice rises, her worry spilling out. "What does that mean? You're not doing something reckless, are you? You don't have to fix this on your own."

"Destiny," Mob-Lee interrupts gently, "this is my family. I have to see it through."

"And what if you get hurt? Or worse?" Her voice cracks. "You think I can just sit here and pretend it's fine?"

Her words hit him harder than he expects. He softens, his voice barely above a whisper. "I got this, Destiny. I promise."

"Don't make promises you can't keep," she replies, her tone heavy with fear.

Inside the hospital, Aura-Lee's phone rings. The number is unknown, but she doesn't hesitate.

"Hello?"

A deep, distorted voice responds, cold and commanding. "Drop the money at Friendship Fountain in one hour. Pick up Robert at Reddie

Point Preserve at the same time. You drop the money, and your brother Mob-Lee picks up Robert. Sending the addresses now."

Aura-Lee's heart pounds in her chest. "Wait—"

"Go alone. Don't be late," the voice cuts her off. The line goes dead.

Her phone vibrates, and two addresses appear on the screen.

Aura-Lee looks up, her face tired but resolute. "Everyone, listen up." She quickly recounts the call, her voice steady despite the dread building inside her.

Mob-Lee and Aura-Lee exchange a glance—silent but understanding. There's no time to waste.

Mob-Lee and Aura-Lee move with purpose, their movements sharp and precise as they prepare for what lies ahead. Every second feels like an eternity, the weight of the situation pressing down on them.

The streets blur as they drive, their minds clouded with fear and a growing sense of impending doom.

Mob-Lee grips the steering wheel tightly. "We'll get him back," he says, to himself.

In the back of her G wagon Aura-Lee stares out the window, her thoughts racing. "Failure isn't an option."

The clock ticks relentlessly, each passing moment bringing them closer to the final showdown—and the unknown.

The Mitchells are out of time. Every move counts, every decision critical as they hurtle toward the point of no return. The fate of their family—and Robert—hangs in the balance.

The moon casts an eerie glow over the fountain, its soothing trickle a stark contrast to the tension in the air. Aura-Lee arrives first, her pulse thrumming as she clutches the duffel bags filled with cash. She scans the desolate park, her instincts sharp and senses on edge.

A man emerges from the shadows, his face obscured by a hood. He steps forward, extending a hand. "Drop the bag and walk away."

Aura-Lee hesitates. "Where's Robert? I need proof he's alive.'

The man doesn't answer. Instead, he pulls out a phone and taps the screen, showing a live feed of Robert, gagged and bloodied, hanging by chains in an open field.

'You'll find him at Reddie Point," the man says "Drop the money, or this ends here."

Aura-Lee places the bag on the ground, her jaw tight with fury. As the man picks it up, she sends a text to Mob-Lee. "The money's gone."

Mob-Lee arrives at the preserve, the silence oppressive as he steps into the shadowy forest. The earpiece Logan gave him crackles with Logan's voice.

"Stay sharp, Mob-Lee. This doesn't feel right.

Mob-Lee moves cautiously, his heart pounding

as he approaches a clearing illuminated by a single floodlight. There, Robert hangs from chains, his head slumped forward.

"Robert!" Mob-Lee sprints forward, his hands working furiously to unshackle his cousin. Robert stirs, groaning weakly.

'Mob-Lee...you shouldn't have come.."

Before Mob-Lee can respond, a sharp whistle pierces the air. He freezes, his blood turning cold as figures emerge from the darkness, guns drawn.

A man steps forward, his face partially illuminated by the harsh light. He smirks.

"You really thought this would end clean?" he sneers. "The money's ours, and so is he"

Mob-Lee places himself between Robert and the men, his fists clenched. "Take the money and walk away. No one has to die tonight."

The man laughs coldly. "Oh, someone's dying tonight. Just not us."

Before Mob-Lee can react, a gunshots ring out The sound is deafening, the flash blinding in the darkness. Mob-Lee turns to see Robert's body jerk violently, blood blossoming across his chest.

"NOOOOO!" Mob-Lee screams, catching his cousin as he slumps forward.

The men open fire, and Mob-Lee dives for
cover, dragging Robert's limp body with him
Bullets tear through the trees, the air thick with
smoke and chaos.

Mob-Lee's mind races as he pulls Robert
deeper into the preserve. Logan's voice crackles in his ear.

'Mob-Lee, what's going on? Talk to me!"

"They shot Robert!" Mob-Lee pants, his voice
raw with grief and fury. "I'm getting him out, but
I need an exit!"

"Head east," Logan replies, his tone urgent. "I'll
meet you at the edge of the preserve.

Mob-Lee presses on, his muscles screaming as
he carries Robert's body. The men are close
behind, their shouts growing louder.

Suddenly, a bullet grazes Mob-Lee's arm, and
he stumbles, nearly dropping Robert. The pain
is sharp, but he forces himself to keep moving

Mob-Lee bursts out of the woodlands, collapsing
beside a waiting car. Logan rushes forward,
helping him lift Robert into the backseat.

Robert's eyes flutter open, his voice barely a
whisper. "Mob… they… They always planned to kill me…they knew…

Mob-Lee grips Robert's hand, his throat

tightening. "Don't talk like that. We're getting you help.'

But Robert's breathing grows shallow, his grip loosening.

"Tell my mom..." Robert's voice trails off as his eyes close.

"No, no, no!" Mob-Lee shakes him, his voice breaking. "Stay with me, Rob! Stay with me!"

Logan places a hand on Mob-Lee's shoulder, his expression grim. "We have to go. Now."

Mob-Lee slumps back, his fists clenched as tears stream down his face. As Logan drives away, the sound of sirens wails in the distance, but it's too late.

The Mitchells have lost one of their own, and the price of their enemies' betrayal is only beginning to unfold.

The loss of Robert sends shockwaves through the Mitchell family, pushing Mob-Lee to the brink. With vengeance burning in his heart, he vows to dismantle the forces that tore his family apart-no matter the cost.

Chapter 8: The Weight of Loss

The church is heavy with silence, save for the soft hum of the organ and the occasional muffled sobs from the mourners. The scent of lilies and roses fills the air, mingling with the weight of grief.

Mob-Lee walks down the aisle with steady but burdened steps, one of the pallbearers carrying Robert Xavier's casket. His hands grip the handle tightly, his knuckles tense. Each step feels like an eternity as he fights back tears, his mind replaying the haunting moments of that night. Watching Robert's body jerk back and forth as bullet tore through his body. The blood. His words. A single tear slowly falls down his right cheek.

Aura-Lee walks behind him, her face set in a mask of sorrow. Camille, dressed in somber black, clutches a handkerchief but hasn't shed a tear, her grief locked behind a stoic exterior. Logan and Vance trail behind, both visibly affected.

As the casket is placed at the front of the church, Mob-Lee catches his reflection in the polished wood—haunted eyes staring back at him, filled with guilt and rage.

The hearse moves slowly, the procession trailing behind. Mob-Lee sits in the back seat of the car, staring out the window. The world outside feels distant, blurred by his inner turmoil.

His mind flashes back to that fateful night: the look in Robert's eyes as he slumped in Mob-Lee's arms, the sound of gunfire echoing in the forest, and the haunting realization that he couldn't save him.

"I should've done more," he thinks, his fists clenching on his lap. "I should've been faster, smarter…something."

Camille sits silently beside him, her gaze fixed on the horizon. She hasn't spoken a word since the night Robert died, her grief an oppressive presence in the car.

The cemetery is quiet, the air heavy with an overcast sky threatening rain. The crowd slowly disperses after the burial, offering hushed condolences to Camille and the family.

As the last of the mourners leave, only Mob-Lee, Aura-Lee, Logan, Camille, and Vance remain. They stand by the grave, the freshly turned earth a stark reminder of their loss.

Camille breaks her week-long silence, her voice cold and resolute. "I want them all dead. I don't care how, and I don't care how long it takes. Every single one of them has to die."

Logan, standing with his arms crossed, nods grimly. "I've already started building a list. I'm gathering intel on everyone who could've been involved."

Vance leans on his cane, his injuries from the shooting still healing. "Everybody dies," he says bitterly. "Even their pets."

Logan sighs, attempting to be the voice of reason. "We need to be smart about this. Revenge is a dish best served with precision, not chaos."

Aura-Lee pulls Mob-Lee aside, her voice low but urgent. "Lee," she says, "I think it's time I told you everything. Like Mom and Dad suggested."

Mob-Lee looks at her sharply. "Everything?"

She nods. "Meet me in the library tonight. I've got some things to show you."

Mob-Lee nods, his face blank. But beneath the surface, a fire of vengeance burns, the weight of guilt pressing down on him like coal under pressure, transforming into something unbreakable.

The ride back is suffocatingly silent. Mob-Lee's phone buzzes constantly, messages of condolences pouring in. Each vibration feels like a jab, a reminder of the life lost.

When Destiny's name flashes on the screen, he hesitates before answering. "Hello."

Her voice is soft, full of concern. "Mob-Lee... I saw you at the service. I didn't want to intrude, but I just wanted to check on you. How are you holding up?"

He closes his eyes, the weight of her question pressing against his chest. "I don't know," he admits, his voice hoarse. "I feel...empty. Guilty. Like I failed him."

"You didn't fail him," she says gently. "You did everything you could. And I know Robert wouldn't want you to carry this guilt. He'd want you to fight, to be strong."

Her words soothe him in a way nothing else has. For a brief moment, the storm in his mind quiets. "Thank you, Destiny," he says quietly.

"Always," she replies. "If you need anything, I'm here."

They end the call, and for the first time in days, Mob-Lee feels a sliver of peace.

The car pulls into the long driveway of the Mitchell estate. Mob-Lee steps out and makes his way to the front steps of the mansion, the grandeur of the estate feeling empty and hollow.

He sits on the steps, staring out at the vast expanse of land. The weight of the past few months crashes over him like a tidal wave. Tears stream down his face, and he doesn't fight them.

Burying his head in his hands, he weeps uncontrollably, the pain and guilt finally breaking free. "I'll make this right," he whispers to himself. "By any means necessary, I'll make them pay."

As the night falls, Mob-Lee's tears dry, replaced by a steely resolve. The fire of vengeance burns brighter than ever, and the weight of his guilt transforms into a weapon.

The Mitchells may have lost Robert, but Mob-Lee vows it won't be in vain. The path ahead is dark and treacherous, but he's ready to walk it.

The Mitchell estate's library is a grand cathedral of knowledge, spanning nearly the size of a public library. Towering bookshelves stretch from floor to ceiling, filled with rare tomes, leather-bound volumes, and artifacts collected over generations. The scent of aged paper and polished wood fills the air. A massive fireplace, its mantel carved with intricate scrollwork, dominates one wall, its flames casting flickering light across the room.

At the center is a vast circular table of ebony wood, surrounded by high-backed chairs. Overhead, a grand chandelier adorned with thousands of crystals refracts light in a dazzling display. Hidden alcoves house antique globes, telescopes, and display cases filled with relics, suggesting the Mitchells' long history of influence and power.

Aura-Lee sits at the head of the table, her face illuminated by the glow of a sleek laptop. Mob-Lee takes the chair opposite her, his posture tense as the weight of the room and the moment presses down on him.

Aura-Lee spins the laptop toward Mob-Lee. "This is everything," she says. The screen displays an elaborate web of names, companies, bank accounts, and associations, each meticulously cataloged.

Mob-Lee's eyes scan the screen, his brow furrowing. "This is everyone," he mutters.

"Everyone in the family," Aura-Lee confirms. "Every business deal, every bank account, every secret they've ever touched."

Before Mob-Lee can fully process the enormity of the information, Aura-Lee reaches beneath the table and slams a stack of folders onto the polished surface. "And this," she says, gesturing to the stack, "is the stuff we don't keep digital copies of. This is yours now, Mob-Lee. All of it."

Mob-Lee frowns. "Why me?"

Aura-Lee responds "this is your role. Protect the family"

Aura-Lee leans forward, her voice dropping to a near whisper. "Did you notice anything missing?"

Mob-Lee scrolls through the database, his expression darkening. "Our files. Yours, mine, Mom's, and Dad's."

"Exactly," she says, her tone sharpening. "We're invisible. Mom and Dad erased us from history. Once they handed over control of Global Strategies, this went into effect. No digital trace. No paper trail. We don't exist."

Mob-Lee leans back in his chair, his mind racing. "What does it mean?"

Aura-Lee's gaze softens slightly. "Dad told me once, he'd been training you your entire life to put this puzzle together. He said when the time came, you'd know exactly what it meant."

Reaching into her pocket, she pulls out a sleek black metal card and slides it across the table. It's weighty, with a microchip embedded in the surface. The letters M.M. and the number 13 are engraved in bold silver.

"This," she says, her voice tinged with amusement, "opens the first door to discovery. Whatever the hell that means."

Mob-Lee picks up the card, examining it closely. The weight of its implications feels heavier than the metal itself.

Aura-Lee chuckles. "Classic Dad, right? Cryptic as hell."

For the first time since Robert's death, Mob-Lee laughs. It's a small, fleeting sound, but it cuts through the oppressive silence.

The moment of levity fades, and Mob-Lee's expression hardens. "Alright, one more thing—where the hell did you get that ransom money so fast?"

Aura-Lee smirks, rising from her seat. "By playing my role in the family."

She heads toward the door, pausing to glance back over her shoulder. "I trust you to figure this out, Mob-Lee. We all do. Now more than ever."

Her words hang in the air like a challenge as she disappears into the dimly lit hallway, leaving Mob-Lee alone with the files, the card, and his thoughts.

Mob-Lee sits in silence, the weight of the moment pressing down on him. He opens one of the folders, flipping through pages of coded messages, offshore account ledgers, and photographs of shadowy figures. Every piece of information feels like a fragment of a larger, more sinister picture.

He picks up the black card again, running his thumb over the engraved letters and number. M.M. 13. What door? What discovery?

As he scans the documents, patterns begin to emerge. Connections between names, locations, and transactions. A coded ledger catches his eye, listing numbered locations. One matches the number on the card.

Outside, thunder rumbles, the storm matching the turmoil within Mob-Lee's mind. His thoughts shift to vengeance. The faces of those responsible for Robert's death flash before him like targets on a shooting range.

He clenches his fists, the fire of revenge burning brighter than ever.

"I'll figure this out," he mutters, his voice low and dangerous. "And I'll make every single one of them pay."

Mob-Lee, seated at the grand table, the storm raging outside. The black card gleams in his hand, a symbol of the dark journey ahead.

Mob-Lee lies on his bed, staring at the intricate coffered ceiling of his room, the ornate patterns illuminated by the moonlight filtering through the curtains. His mind drifts to memories of his father, Deacon Mitchell, a man whose lessons always seemed layered with meaning.

Deacon's voice echoes in his mind, calm yet commanding:

"Mob, playing your part isn't about pretending—it's about strategy. The world's a chessboard. Never let anyone see your next move."

"Integrity doesn't mean being soft. It means staying true to your mission, no matter how hard it gets. Always remember: loyalty to family, loyalty to the plan."

Suddenly, a particular conversation surfaces—a moment that now feels pivotal.

10 Years Earlier

Fifteen-year-old Mob-Lee stands in his room, shoving clothes into a military-issued duffle bag. His jaw is clenched, his movements sharp and frustrated. Behind him, Deacon leans against the doorframe, his arms crossed, a faint smile playing on his lips.

"This isn't a punishment," Deacon says evenly. "This is a lesson in discipline."

Mob-Lee spins around, his eyes blazing. "I was defending myself!"

Deacon nods slowly. "I know."

The memory sharpens, replaying the fight in Mob-Lee's mind: the bully's taunts, the months of torment, the moment he'd snapped. His training had taken over—three precise moves, a broken arm, jaw, and nose. The bully hadn't stood a chance.

Deacon steps into the room. "But you have to think more methodically about these types of things, Mob. You don't just react—you plan. Every action, every move has a ripple effect."

Mob-Lee slings the bag over his shoulder, his defiance unwavering. "So, what am I supposed to do? Let people walk all over me?"

Deacon places a firm hand on his son's shoulder. "No. But ask yourself this: What would you do if you were invisible? Would you let it go or go after them in your own time?"

The question lingers in the air. Mob-Lee frowns, the sharpness in his eyes giving way to confusion. "I'd destroy them on my time," he mutters.

Deacon chuckles softly, stepping back toward the door. "Good. Remember that."

The memory jolts Mob-Lee upright in bed, his chest heaving as if he'd just emerged from a dream. His father's words echo in his mind: What would you do if you were invisible?

"I'd destroy them," Mob-Lee whispers, his voice steady this time.

The pieces begin to click into place. The files, the black card, the erased histories—they weren't just tools for protection. They were weapons. Weapons meant to dismantle enemies from the shadows.

His thoughts swirl, connecting threads of his family's secrets and Robert's death. His fists clench. "I'm supposed to use this to destroy them," he says aloud, his tone filled with determination. "All of them."

Elsewhere, in the grittiest part of the city known as "The Bottom," a block party rages. It's been an all-day event, and the streets are alive with celebration. Music thunders from massive speakers, and the scent of barbecue wafts through the air.

TopBoy, the neighborhood kingpin, walks among the crowd, handing out cash like the ghetto's Santa Claus. Children laugh, mothers thank him, and the Boys from The Bottom cheer.

"This is for the biggest lick of all time!" TopBoy shouts, holding up a glass of champagne.

Luxury cars line the streets, their doors open as music blasts. The duffle bags of cash are stacked in plain view, a trophy for their audacious heist.

A lone car creeps through the chaos, its tinted windows masking the occupants inside. Behind the wheel is a stoic driver. In the back seat, Vance Cruz sits silently, a camera in hand.

He snaps photo after photo, capturing every detail: the duffle bags, the cash, TopBoy's grin. He lowers the camera, his jaw tightening.

"I see you," Vance murmurs, his voice laced with venom. He places the camera down, the weight of rage settling in his chest.

Vance pulls out his phone and types a quick message to Aura-Lee:

Vance: Just like you said. The money is here, and they're not even trying to hide it.

A reply buzzes almost instantly:

Aura-Lee: OK. So now we know exactly how to play this.

Unbeknownst to TopBoy, a tracker stitched into the duffle bag's handle has already revealed his location.

As the car pulls away from the festivities, Vance smiles to himself, the kind of smile that promises retribution.

The morning sun rises, casting a golden glow over the city as Mob-Lee drives along a deserted coastal road. His destination is based the files he reviewed: an abandoned scuba diving instruction school at the edge of town. The air is crisp, but Mob-Lee feels a mix of anticipation and unease as he pulls into the gravel parking lot.

The building is derelict, its windows boarded up and its exterior weathered by years of neglect. A faded sign reads "Discovery Dive Center" with the faint outline of a "13" painted on the side.

Mob-Lee parks his car and steps out, scanning the area. He pulls his jacket tighter against the morning chill and makes his way to a boarded window. After a brief search, he pries the boards loose and slips inside.

The air inside smells of saltwater and mildew. Mob-Lee navigates through the dusty interior, his footsteps echoing in the empty halls. Rusted scuba tanks and broken diving masks litter the floor, remnants of the school's past life.

After 30 minutes of searching, he stumbles upon a small back office. Papers and faded maps clutter the desk, and a corkboard hangs on the wall, covered in old photographs and notes.

One picture catches his eye: his father, Deacon, standing beside another man who looks vaguely familiar. They're posed in front of a sleek matte black speedboat, its side emblazoned with the word Discovery and the number 13.

Mob-Lee pulls the picture down, inspecting it closely. His heart races as he shoves it into his pocket. Behind where the picture had hung, he notices something unusual: a small metal square embedded in the wall, with a thin slit at its center.
The letters M.M. engraved in the face.

Mob-Lee takes the black card from his pocket, turning it over in his hand. Is this what it's for? he wonders.

He hesitates, then slides the card into the slit. A mechanical hiss echoes through the room. Startled, Mob-Lee steps back as a hidden wall panel slides away to the right, revealing a staircase descending into darkness.

Adrenaline coursing through him, Mob-Lee cautiously steps onto the staircase. The air grows cooler as he descends, the sound of the sliding wall sealing him inside. At the bottom, lights flicker to life, illuminating a vast underground command center.

Mob-Lee stands in awe, taking in the scene before him. The room is massive, lined with steel walls and high-tech equipment. It's part armory, part surveillance hub, part tactical operations center.

An array of weapons is displayed on the walls—pistols, rifles, knives, even experimental gadgets Mob-Lee has never seen before. A small gun range occupies one corner, while tactical vehicles and armored uniforms line another. Monitors flicker with surveillance feeds, maps, and encrypted data streams.

Mob-Lee runs his hand over a dusty table, blowing off years of neglect. He spots a storage container marked Grenades. Hesitantly, he opens it, pulling out a small grenade. He turns it over in his hand, a wry smile spreading across his face.

"The Door to Discovery," he whispers. "What were you up to, Dad?"

Mob-Lee sits at a central workstation, the black card still in his hand. His mind races with possibilities. This was my father's legacy, he thinks. But why didn't he tell me?

He pulls out his phone, typing a quick message to Aura-Lee:

Mob-Lee: I have something you have got to see.

He presses send. Message failed.

Frowning, he tries again. Message failed.

Mob-Lee stares at his phone, then glances around the room. A sense of clarity washes over him. Maybe this isn't meant to be shared. Not yet.

He slides the phone back into his pocket and leans back in the chair, gripping the grenade tightly. The thrill of discovery mingles with the burning desire for revenge.

"This is my secret now," he murmurs.

Mob-Lee's mind churns with plans, his path forward now clearer than ever.

In an old, dilapidated house on a forgotten side street in the Bottom, TopBoy gathers his Shottas in the dimly lit living room. The air smells of sweat, stale beer, and cigarettes. The walls are peeling, and the floor creaks under the weight of the gang's restless energy.

The young men are still high off their success. They'd pulled off what no one else dared—a $10 million ransom, a crippling blow to their opposition, and a clear message to the city: the Bottom was rising.

TopBoy, leaning against a scarred table, scans the room. His piercing gaze commands silence as he speaks.

TopBoy: "Alright, boys, it's time to step up. We didn't come this far to stop now."

He pulls out a duffle bag, unzips it, and tosses wads of cash onto the table.

TopBoy: "We're gonna flood the streets. From now on, everything moves through us. This city's gonna eat, sleep, and breathe the Bottom."

The Shottas cheer, but TopBoy silences them with a raised hand.

TopBoy: "This ain't time to celebrate. Not yet…BabyBoy!"

Shawn, aka BabyBoy, steps forward.

TopBoy: (throws $100,000 in cash) "Get us armed. Now. Once word gets out we're the new crew, every enemy we got is gonna come for us. We need firepower and we need it fast."

A moment of unease washes over TopBoy as he says the words. His gut tightens, but he shakes it off. No time for doubts, he thinks. We're too far in.

Outside, the streets are eerily silent, a stark contrast to the chaos and celebration from the previous night. A golden Buick sits parked in front of the house, its polished surface gleaming under the faint morning light.

Unbeknownst to the Shottas inside, Vance cruises by in a black SUV. His driver slows the car as Vance snaps pictures through the tinted window, focusing on the Buick.

Vance smirks, his fingers flying over his phone.

Vance (texting the family group chat): Anybody recognize this?

Back at the Mitchell estate, phones buzz as the family group chat lights up.

Mob-Lee: Yeah, it was there that night at Reddie Point.

A pause.

Logan: Yeah, it was in the front yard the night I went to talk to "TopBoy"... or should I say Junior? (adds a laughing emoji)

Vance grins as he reads Logan's response.

Vance: Good to know. We'll track this car.

Vance's driver pulls the SUV over a block away. Slipping out of the car, the man moves swiftly and silently. He crouches beside the golden Buick, pulling a small GPS tracker from his pocket.

With practiced precision, he attaches the tracker under the wheel well. He stands, glancing around to ensure he wasn't noticed, then slips back into the SUV.

As the car pulls away, the driver speaks.

Driver: "You think they'll catch on?"

Vance: (smirks) "Doesn't matter if they do. We've got what we need."

The SUV disappears into the distance.

Inside the house, TopBoy finishes laying out the next steps. The Shottas nod, energized by the promise of power and control.

But outside, the silence seems heavier now, as if the air itself is watching. The golden Buick sits unguarded, its new passenger—a GPS tracker—ready to lead the Mitchells straight to the Bottom.

TopBoy pauses, his instincts screaming that something isn't right. He glances at the window but shakes his head. Paranoia's a weakness, he thinks.

Meanwhile, back at the Mitchell estate, Mob-Lee stares at his phone, piecing together Vance's clues. His mind races. The Buick. Reddie Point. TopBoy.

Aura-Lee, reading the same texts, picks up her laptop.

Aura-Lee: "We've got them now. Let's make this count."

Mob-Lee nods, his expression dark.

Mob-Lee: "This isn't just about tracking them. It's about sending a message. The Bottom's about to learn what happens when they mess with us."

BFTB Shottas plan as the Mitchells prepare their next move.an explosive confrontation looming on the horizon.

Chapter 9: Follow my lead

The Mitchell estate library hums with quiet urgency. Rows of ancient books line the shelves, but the central table is a modern war room. Aura-Lee sits at her laptop, her sharp eyes scanning the GPS map. She marks the Buick's stops with precision, her fingers flying over the keyboard as she cross-references locations.

Aura-Lee: (to herself) "Another stop… Market Street. That's three suppliers in one day."

Her tone is cold, calculating. She leans back, studying the marked map on the large display screen. Each pin represents a potential target.

Aura-Lee: "Everything they've built, everything they will build. It's all here."

Behind her, Logan sits at a desk stacked with papers and files. He's compiling profiles of every member of the Boys From The Bottom (BFTB), from the lowest runners to their leader, Kevin Marks Junior—TopBoy.

Logan: (calling out) "Mob-Lee, come here."

Mob-Lee, leaning against a bookshelf, walks over.

Logan: "Do you know a Kevin Marks?"

The name hits Mob-Lee like a thunderclap.

Mob-Lee: (frowning) "Yeah, I know that bitch. Why?"

Logan: "That's TopBoy."

The room falls deathly silent. Mob-Lee stares at Logan, the weight of the revelation sinking in. Memories flood back—a bloody fistfight, the crunch of bone, and the fury that sent him to military school.

Mob-Lee: "That's the boy I fought before I got sent away."

Aura-Lee, sitting at her laptop, freezes.

Aura-Lee: "Really? Do you think he knows it's you?"

Mob-Lee nods grimly.

Mob-Lee: "He has to. He had to have seen me that night, but I didn't see his face."

The room grows tense as the implications settle in.

Logan: "You think this is his revenge? Ten years holding onto that grudge?"

Mob-Lee: (scoffs) "No! But Sheesh. If that's the case, he's about to get what he's been asking for."

Vance, sitting quietly in the corner, speaks up, his voice cutting through the tension.

Vance: "So you're telling me this dude killed my brother because you beat him up ten years ago?"

The room goes silent again. Logan shakes his head.

Logan: "I don't think that's the whole reason, but it could definitely be a piece of it. A grudge like that can turn into a vendetta."

Mob-Lee's fists clench at his sides, a storm of emotions brewing inside him. Rage, guilt, and determination swirl as he processes the connection. He reaches into his pocket and places the grenade he found in the Discovery hideout onto the table.

The room collectively stiffens, eyes widening in shock.

Aura-Lee: "Mob-Lee…"

Mob-Lee: (calmly, cryptically) "The door of Discovery."

Mob-Lee turns to Aura-Lee.

Mob-Lee: "Where's the car now?"

Aura-Lee glances at the GPS screen.

Aura-Lee: "Monaco Arms."

Mob-Lee grabs the grenade and his coat, his face a mask of cold fury.

Mob-Lee: "Watch the news."

Before anyone can respond, he's out the door, his boots echoing down the marble hallway.

Outside, Mob-Lee gets into the sleek black Bentley and speeds off, the engine roaring as he tears down the estate's driveway. His mind races as fast as the car.

"He killed Robert. All of this… for what? A fight? A decade of hate? He's gonna learn today."

Back in the library, the family scrambles.

Aura-Lee: "We can't let him do this alone."

Logan: "If we stop him now, we risk tipping off TopBoy. This has to play out."

Vance grips the edge of the table, his jaw tight.
Vance: "If Mob-Lee gets himself killed over this, it's on us."

Mob-Lee's Bentley weaves through traffic, heading towards Monaco Arms. His grip tightens on the wheel as his eyes burn with focus.

"No more waiting. No more games. This ends tonight."

The grenade resting in his lap, and the tension crackling like static in the air.

TopBoy slouches on the threadbare couch in a rundown house in the Bottom, the faint sounds of the neighborhood bleeding through the thin walls—yelling kids, distant sirens, the occasional car rumbling past. He looks down at his phone as a text comes through:

"Waiting on them to load up and then headed to the spot."

A sly grin spreads across his face. This re-up was exactly what he needed to solidify his control. It was the kind of move that could shift BFTB's standing from a local crew to a dominant force. As he leans back, his mind drifts to grander visions: high rises, yachts, luxury suits—him, a modern Tony Montana, untouchable and unstoppable.

He pulls out a second phone, thumbing through the contacts until he lands on his sister's number. "Grab something to eat later, sis?" he types quickly. A reply buzzes in almost instantly: "Yeah, I'll be free around 5pm. Wanna meet at Blue Boys Diner?"

"Bet," he responds, smirking. She always made time for him, no matter how crazy life got.

TopBoy stands, pacing the small living room. His ambition feels too big for the confines of this house, this neighborhood, even this life. Every memory fuels the fire inside him—his dad being hauled off to prison, the foster homes, the fights that taught him survival, the bullet scars that proved his resilience.

He remembers Robert Xavier. The deal that could've changed everything.

The promise of a seat at the table, a way out. He clenches his fists, jaw tightening as he recalls Robert's smug grin and casual dismissal of his lost investment. Black Sky wasn't going to merge; Robert's words had been clear. But it wasn't just the money—it was the disrespect.

"I'll wipe that smile off your face permanently," he had warned Robert. And he meant it.

The memory lingers like a bad taste as TopBoy replays that night in his head—the chaos after Vance's attack, the split-second decisions that led to Robert's abduction. It wasn't supposed to go down like that, but TopBoy had adjusted, adapted, and taken control.

The ransom had been a power move, but Robert's fate was already sealed. Even with the payout, TopBoy felt justified. The streets didn't allow second chances.

His phone buzzes again, snapping him out of his thoughts. "We're leaving in about 20 minutes."

"Time to get it," TopBoy mutters, grabbing his jacket. He tucks his gun into his waistband, checks himself in the cracked mirror, and steps out into the humid air of the Bottom.

Mob-Lee sits in his car, engine off, in the shadow of a laundromat's dim security light. From here, he has a clear view of the Monaco Arms complex. His eyes lock onto the gold Buick parked in front of one of the apartments.

The car fits the description perfectly—gold rims, tinted windows, and an air of arrogance that makes it stand out like a sore thumb. Four figures sit inside, their silhouettes barely visible through the glass.

Mob-Lee takes a deep breath, steadying himself. This is about sending a message.

"Now or never," he mutters, stepping out of his vehicle.

The walk toward the Buick feels longer than it is, every step deliberate. Mob-Lee's eyes stay on the car, his peripheral vision scanning for potential threats. He counts two additional figures standing near the entrance to the apartment building, their postures relaxed but their hands close to their sides.

The gold Buick shifts slightly as someone inside adjusts their position. Mob-Lee stops about ten feet away, his presence unmistakable now.

The driver rolls down the window just enough for a voice to slip through.

"What you want, big man?" one of the shottas asks, his tone sharp but cautious.

Mob-Lee smirks. "Business."

The word hangs in the air, heavy with meaning. For a moment, the only sound is the faint hum of the Buick's engine and the distant noise of the streets.

"You sure you in the right place for that?" the shotta retorts.

Mob-Lee steps closer, his confidence unshaken. "I'm exactly where I need to be."

The tension thickens, a silent standoff building as both sides assess the other. Mob-Lee's hand stays loose by his side, ready to act but waiting for the right moment.

The next move will decide everything.

Mob-Lee stands frozen in the shadows outside the gold Buick, his silhouette barely visible beneath the dim light spilling from the apartments of Monaco Arms. His heartbeat thuds in his chest, the weight of the moment settling on him like a stormcloud. The cold night air stings his skin as he waits, his gaze fixed on the car, every muscle in his body taut with anticipation. This is the moment.

The window rolls down a little more, the sound of the glass sliding on metal a harsh, grating noise in the otherwise still air. A stream of cigarette smoke billows out, and the driver's low chuckle drifts across the distance.

One of the men in the back seat leans forward, squinting through the haze of smoke and the darkness at Mob-Lee. "Okay, what kinda business you got, fam?" he asks, his voice thick with suspicion, though laced with curiosity.

Mob-Lee stands taller, his eyes cold but his expression steady. "I'm tryin' to get a ball," he says, the words deliberate, carrying an edge that suggests this isn't just an ordinary transaction.

The car erupts in laughter.

One of the men, sitting on the far side, lets out a boisterous laugh, slapping his knee. "This boy tryin' to get an eighth?" he mocks, his voice dripping with amusement, dismissing Mob-Lee's request outright.

Another man, leaning casually against the door, rolls his eyes. "Tell this man to run along. BFTB doesn't deal in petty sacks anymore."

The driver takes another drag from his cigarette and blows the smoke directly in Mob-Lee's direction, laughing under his breath. "Run along, kid. Ain't no room for you here," he says, his tone patronizing, almost a taunt.

Mob-Lee's eyes narrow, but he doesn't let their words rattle him. Instead, a cold, calculated calm washes over him. Now or never—he whispers the words to himself, a mantra.

He reaches into his pocket, He knows this is the right move. His heart beats faster now, but his mind is sharp.

Mob-Lee pulls the grenade from his pocket, feeling its weight in his hand, the tension rising. As the window creaks down another inch, just enough to slip the object inside, Mob-Lee steps forward, moving like a shadow. His movements are swift, deliberate. He doesn't hesitate.

"Catch!" he says, the words cool, calculated. He tosses the grenade through the gap in the window just as the men in the car start to react.

The grenade clinks against the edge of the window as it falls inside, the sound too loud in the quiet night. The men inside the Buick scramble, yelling, fumbling with the object, the windows and the door handles, but they're too slow. The doors are locked. Panic fills the car as they try to open the window, but it's already too late.

Mob-Lee doesn't look back. He hears the commotion behind him, the chaos of the men struggling to escape, but he keeps moving, jogging briskly toward the laundromat. His steps are measured, his heart pounding in his chest. He knows he has seconds before the explosion—seconds that feel like hours.

Then, the night is split by a blinding flash of light. A deafening roar follows immediately, shaking the ground beneath him. The explosion is so intense that it feels like the world has cracked open, the fireball shooting up into the sky, lighting up the darkness.

Mob-Lee's body tenses as the shockwave hits him, the heat from the blast searing his skin even from a distance. The explosion sends a shower of sparks and debris into the air, the Buick's metal twisting and crumpling as if it were paper. Glass shatters in all directions, the sharp sound of breaking windows ringing in the air.

The fireball consumes the car in an instant, turning it into a mass of flames and twisted wreckage. The force of the explosion is so powerful that the night sky flickers for a moment, a harsh, fiery glow taking over the street. The air smells of burning rubber and gasoline, thick and acrid.

Mob-Lee doesn't stop to watch the aftermath. He's already moving faster now, his feet pounding the pavement as the explosion reverberates through the streets.

Inside the laundromat, Mob-Lee finds a brief moment of respite. The sound of the explosion still echoes in his ears, his heart hammering in his chest. He presses his back against the wall, exhaling slowly, trying to calm his racing thoughts. He can feel the heat from the blast still radiating in the air, even from inside the building.

Through the small window, he sees the smoke rising, thick and black, curling up into the sky. The sirens are already starting to wail in the distance, but Mob-Lee knows he's got time. For now, he's safe. For now.

He pulls out his phone, his fingers shaking slightly as he checks for any new messages. Aunt Camille's name flashes on the screen.

Where are you?

Mob-Lee doesn't reply immediately. His mind races, planning his next move. He knows this is only the beginning—the explosion was a message, a signal. BFTB will be looking for retaliation, but Mob-Lee has his sights set on something bigger now.

Mob-Lee slips out the back of the laundromat, his eyes scanning the dark alley before him. The streets are quieter now, but there's an undercurrent of tension in the air. The blast has done its job, but the game is far from over.

He pulls his jacket tighter around him, adjusting his hood to keep a low profile. The night has taken on a different tone now—dangerous, charged with the promise of violence.

As Mob-Lee disappears into the shadows, his phone buzzes once again. It's Aunt Camille.

I need to see you. Immediately.

Mob-Lee's lips curl into a faint smile, but it's the kind of smile that holds no warmth. He tucks the phone back into his pocket and walks around the building to his car, the sounds of sirens and distant chaos fading behind him.

The streets may be full of whispers now, but soon, everyone will know that someone has made their mark. And nothing will be the same again.

The Blue Boys Diner buzzes softly with the hum of a jukebox in the corner and the occasional clink of dishes from the kitchen. Kevin sits alone in his usual booth, one hand idly tapping the edge of the table while the other scrolls through his phone. He checks the time. Early again, as always.

A text pops up, and he quickly types a reply to BabyBoy.

"Everything handled?"

Satisfied, Kevin leans back, watching the light filter through the blinds. The TV mounted on the wall above the counter flickers, catching his attention.

"Breaking news: Explosion on Jacksonville's Northside. More details at 5."

Kevin narrows his eyes slightly, his mind churning for a moment before he shakes it off.

At exactly 5:00 p.m., the bell above the diner door jingles. Kevin's face softens as he stands, his guarded demeanor giving way to a genuine warmth.

"Kevin!" His sister exclaims, her voice carrying across the room.

"D-Nice!" he responds, grinning as they embrace tightly.

The two slide into the booth, Kevin motioning for the waitress to come over. Their connection is effortless, their conversation flowing naturally as they order.

The news segment resumes, drawing Kevin's gaze to the screen.

"Breaking news: A car explosion at Monaco Arms apartments on Jacksonville's Northside has left four dead. Police are on the scene, and foul play is suspected. More updates as we get information."

Kevin's stomach twists, a chill creeping up his spine. His eyes flicker briefly with concern before he smooths his expression.

"You good?" she asks, tilting her head.

Kevin nods quickly, brushing it off. "Yeah, I'm good. Just a lot on my plate, you know?"

She doesn't push further, shifting the conversation back to their meal.

The two reminisce, sharing stories and laughs, their bond evident in the way they speak. It's been months since they last saw each other, and the time apart melts away as they fall into an easy rhythm.

"How's everything going with the new project?" Kevin asks, genuinely curious.

"Busy, but it's all coming together," she says with a smile. "I'm making moves, Kev. You'd be proud."

"I already am," Kevin replies, his voice soft but firm.

Her eyes glimmer with appreciation, and for a moment, Kevin feels a rare peace, even as the news lingers at the back of his mind.

Outside, the air is cool, a light breeze rustling through the street as they stand near her car. Kevin pulls her into a hug, holding her close.

"You ever need anything, just call me," he says quietly, his voice filled with unspoken emotion.

She nods, smiling warmly. "Same goes for you."

He replies "I got you, Destiny."

Kevin watches as she drives off, the taillights disappearing into the distance. For a brief moment, the weight on his shoulders lightens.

His phone buzzes in his pocket, snapping him back to reality. He reads the message from BabyBoy:

"Big problem, Top. Call me."

Kevin exhales sharply, dialing the number without hesitation. BabyBoy picks up immediately.

"I know," Kevin says before BabyBoy can speak. "I'm on the way."

Sliding into his car, Kevin grips the wheel tightly. His mind races as the engine roars to life, the weight of the explosion settling heavily on him.

Mob-Lee pulls into the driveway of the Mitchell estate, the gravel crunching beneath the tires of his car. The sprawling mansion looms in the distance, its columns and stately presence as imposing as always. A single black sedan is parked in the driveway, its tinted windows reflecting the early evening sky. Mob-Lee feels a subtle unease ripple through him, but he suppresses it, stepping out of the car and heading for the front door.

Inside the parlor, the atmosphere is thick with tension. Aunt Camille, ever poised, sits across from two unfamiliar faces. A man and a woman, both dressed in dark suits, their expressions serious. The woman's sharp features and cold eyes catch Mob-Lee's attention immediately. He doesn't like the look of them, but he remains composed as he steps into the room.

"Mob-Lee," Aunt Camille's voice rings out, warm yet businesslike. "This is Agent Taylor and Agent Alvarez of the FBI."

Mob-Lee steps forward, offering a firm handshake to both agents, his expression neutral. "Good evening. How may I help you?" His voice is calm, but his mind races with curiosity.

Agent Taylor, the blonde woman with stringy hair that looks like it's been pulled too tight, doesn't waste any time. Her blue eyes are hard, her face set in a permanent scowl that makes her look older than she really is. She cuts straight to the point.

"We're looking into some questionable activities at Global Strategies," Agent Taylor says, her voice clipped and authoritative. "We'd like to ask you a few questions."

Mob-Lee's brow furrows slightly, but he quickly masks any sign of concern. "I just recently inherited the company," he replies smoothly. "I'd advise you to speak to Global Strategies' legal team. I'm not involved in the day-to-day operations."

Agent Alvarez, a stockier man with dark hair and a tight jaw, tries to continue the conversation. "We understand, Mr. Mitchell, but we're hoping to clarify a few things—"

Before he can finish, Aunt Camille interrupts, her voice commanding but with a touch of warmth. "Agent Alvarez, I believe my nephew has made his position clear," she says. "We're fully aware of the legal process here, and I trust you'll respect that."

The tension in the room thickens, but Aunt Camille's authority is undeniable. The agents exchange a brief, unreadable glance, then nod curtly, sensing that pushing further would be unwise.

In the background, the television plays softly, the 7 p.m. news anchoring the atmosphere with its stark updates. The camera cuts to a breaking news segment that immediately captures Mob-Lee's attention.

"Breaking news," the anchor's voice rings out, her tone grim. "A car explosion on Jacksonville's Northside, Monaco Arms apartments, has left four dead. No additional injuries, no leads or suspects at this time. Police are on the scene and will continue their investigation. We will keep you updated."

Mob-Lee's stomach tightens at the mention of the explosion. His eyes flicker toward the screen, but he quickly averts his gaze as the agents exchange brief glances.

Mob-Lee rises from his chair, his movements measured as he escorts the agents to the door. The atmosphere is tense, thick with unspoken questions. As he closes the door behind them, he turns around and is met with a penetrating silence.

Vance, Logan, Aura-Lee, and Camille all stand in the foyer, watching him with expressions ranging from suspicion to amusement. Aura-Lee, her eyes sharp with concern, steps forward first.

"Mob-Lee, what did you do?" she asks, her voice a mix of disbelief and concern. Her brow is furrowed, and her arms are crossed, waiting for an explanation.

Vance, on the other hand, has a wide grin plastered across his face, clearly amused by the situation. His smile is too broad, too knowing. He waits, eyes gleaming, anticipating Mob-Lee's response.

Camille, ever the composed figure, speaks last, her voice laced with a hint of affection. "I can't hear your answer, but just know I love you." She smiles softly, her gaze warm but guarded.

Logan, who's been standing off to the side, his arms crossed, breaks the tension with a single question, his voice low but curious. "Broad day?"

Mob-Lee stands tall, meeting each of their gazes in turn, before a relaxed smile slowly spreads across his face. He takes a deep breath, his shoulders easing as the weight of the situation seems to lift.

"Did you catch the news?" Mob-Lee asks, his voice cool, almost nonchalant, despite the tension in the room. His eyes flicker toward the television screen, knowing they've all seen it. The explosion was his message—one that he's confident will speak louder than any words ever could.

Chapter 10 - Thr Fallout

The sun barely rises above the city skyline as Agent Taylor and Agent Alvarez stride into the grand lobby of the Global Strategies headquarters. The air is crisp with early-morning efficiency, the building already humming with the quiet buzz of employees starting their day. Taylor, her expression severe, clutches a warrant in her gloved hands, while Alvarez scans the area, his sharp eyes missing nothing.

"We need to speak with the person in charge of operations," Taylor announces to the receptionist, her tone leaving no room for debate.

Moments later, Tasha Sinclair appears, dressed impeccably in a navy-blue power suit that does little to hide the tension in her shoulders. Her polished demeanor falters slightly as Taylor holds up the warrant.

"We're here to seize all computers, records, and pertinent files for analysis," Taylor states firmly. "Please lead the way."

Tasha hesitates, her mind racing. "Of course, right this way," she says, forcing a smile.

As they walk through the corridors of Global Strategies, Tasha's heels click against the pristine marble floors, echoing ominously in the silence. Her mind churns as she glances at her staff. Each face she passes belongs to someone she thought she could trust, and she has no choice but to rely on that trust now.

In a low, almost imperceptible voice, she utters phrases that seem harmless to the agents but carry a deadly meaning to her team.

"Linda continue to Review Project Horizon."
"Dave Revisit Protocol 7."
"Grace check to see if they've Implemented the Phoenix Directive."

Her employees' expressions barely change, but subtle movements ripple through the office. Fingers hover over keyboards, shredders hum faintly to life, and files begin to disappear into locked cabinets. The building seems to pulse with quiet panic, though outwardly, everything remains eerily calm.

The agents' keen eyes dart around, picking up on the tension in the air. Taylor whispers to Alvarez, "They're hiding something. Watch them."

As they move deeper into the headquarters, a side office catches Alvarez's attention. Behind a glass wall, a man feverishly types at a computer, his fingers flying over the keyboard. The sound of the hard drive's frantic whirring is unmistakable.

"Stop what you're doing and step away from the computer," Alvarez orders, hand on his firearm stepping into the room.

The man freezes, his eyes darting to Tasha, who stands nearby.

"Everyone, stop what you're doing immediately," Taylor commands loudly, her voice cutting through the office noise. "Exit the building."

Employees begin to rise from their desks, their faces etched with guilt, fear, or both. Tasha clenches her fists, her polished mask beginning to crack under the pressure.

In the conference room, Tasha sits under the bright, sterile lights, her composure unraveling. Her usual confidence feels like a distant memory as Taylor and Alvarez fire off question after question.

"Let's talk about the movement of assets from Black Sky to ValorTech," Taylor begins, her piercing blue eyes locked onto Tasha.

Alvarez leans forward, his voice quieter but no less intense. "And the recent firing of the Black Sky board. What can you tell us about that?"

Tasha stammers, her fingers gripping the edge of the table. "I—I'm not directly involved in every decision made by the board or the parent company. You'd have to ask..."

"How about the kidnapping and murder of Robert Xavier Mitchell?" Taylor interrupts, her tone icy. "Or the shooting of Vance Cruz?"

Tasha feels her throat tighten, her heart pounding in her chest. Every question feels like another thread unraveling the tightly woven fabric of her life. She struggles to find answers that won't implicate her or expose the company.

The door opens abruptly, and Global Strategies' legal team strides in, their faces a mixture of determination and disdain.

"This questioning is over," says the lead attorney, placing a hand on Tasha's shoulder. "Ms. Sinclair will not be answering any further questions today."

As Tasha is escorted out of the room, her mind whirls with conflicting thoughts. Her phone feels heavy in her pocket, a lifeline to two people she isn't sure she can face.

Her first instinct is to call Brandon, her fiancé and CEO of ValorTech, to warn him about the investigation. She imagines his voice on the other end, calm and calculating as always, ready with a plan.

But then her thoughts drift to Mob-Lee, her ex-fiancé and now her boss. Would he see this as her failure? Would he stand by her or turn his back?

Around her, the chaos is deafening. Agents haul out computers and hard drives, filling boxes with documents. Employees stand by the elevators, whispering nervously. A shredder in the corner office sits jammed, its motor whining faintly. The air smells faintly of burnt plastic and anxiety.

Tasha's polished exterior is gone, replaced by the trembling uncertainty of a woman who knows her carefully constructed world is crumbling.

As she steps outside, the sunlight feels harsh and unforgiving. Her hands shake as she pulls out her phone. Her thumb hovers over two names in her contact list.

Brandon Corvin.
Mob-Lee Mitchell.

Her chest tightens as she presses the screen, her decision made.

Detective Aiden Finn flicks the last drag of his cigarette across the cracked asphalt, stepping under the fluttering police tape with a sigh. The acrid stench of burned fuel and scorched metal hangs heavy in the air, mixing with the distant hum of early morning traffic

"A fucking grenade?" Finn mutters, his tone a mix of disbelief and frustration as he approaches a knot of uniformed officers near the charred remains of a sedan

"Yes, Detective," one of the officers replies grimly. "Thrown into the passenger side window. Shrapnel blew out the entire interior.

Finn narrows his eyes, stepping closer to the vehicle. The car's shell is barely intact, the windows blown out, jagged glass scattered across the pavement. Black scorch marks fan out from the epicenter of the explosion, and pieces of twisted metal are embedded in the walls of the adjacent apartment complex.

Another officer steps forward with a clipboard "Here's what forensics has so far:

The grenade detonated in the front passenger seat, based on the blast pattern

Shrapnel perforated the car's frame and tore through the victims at close range.

The bodies were found in the vehicle, though two victims were partially ejected due to the force of the explosion

Primary cause of death: severe trauma from shrapnel and the blast wave. Burn injuries secondary."

Finn listens, his sharp eyes scanning the scene
Body parts and Blood spatters stain the pavement around the car, a grim testament to the violence. The scent of burned flesh lingers, almost making him gag, but he swallows the urge

"What about witnesses?" Finn asks, though he already knows the answer.

"Nothing," the officer responds. "Nobody saw anything. Or they're too scared to talk."

Finn glances at the mangled bodies as crime scene technicians work to document the scene Though the victims haven't been formally identified, the car itself is unmistakable.

'BFTB," Finn mutters, shaking his head. "Boys from the bottom I'd bet my badge."

Officer Furman approaches, offering a tired smile as he extends his hand.

"Fancy running into you so soon," Finn greets, shaking Furman's hand firmly.

"What do we have?"

Furman grimaces. "The usual nobody's seen anything. A gang car bombed. No cameras at the scene, but we're pulling footage from nearby intersections and stores. Might get lucky.'

Finn leans in, lowering his voice. "Let's talk victims. I know this crew.

Finn points to each body in turn, rattling off their criminal profiles.

Victim 1. Tyrone "T-Rex" Carter

Enforcer for BTFB.
Known for his brutal methods-
arrests include assault with a deadly weapon and multiple aggravated assaults.

Recently linked to a bloody dispute over control of a drug corridor.

2. DeShawn "Shawnie B" Brooks

Mid-level operator and narcotics distributor.

Arrest record includes possession with intent to distribute and trafficking firearms

Known for his paranoia and habit of rotating vehicles to avoid detection.

"Bet he wishes he had switched cars today" Furman says.

3. Jamal "Ghost" Harris

Specialist in vehicle theft and high-speed escapes

Clean arrest record, but numerous sightings at crime scenes

Rumored to be the crew's main getaway driver.

4. Lorenzo "Low-Key" Alvarez

Planner and strategist for BTFB.
The quiet one with a head for logistics. Suspected of organizing a multi-state drug pipeline

"They were dirty," Finn says, his voice low. "But even for them, this is a messy way to go."

Furman nods thoughtfully. "Can you think of anyone who'd go this far? A grenade... that's not your average gang spat."

"Not yet," Finn admits. "But something about

this feels personal. It's too bold. Someone wanted this to make a statement.

Furman shifts uncomfortably. He shifts thought to back when he first worked with detective Finn "what happened with the Cruz kid's case."

Finn's jaw tightens. "Vance Cruz? That case is still open.'

"Hmmm," Furman says, crossing his arms, "this all started around the same time, didn't it? Vance gets shot at the merger celebration, and now we've got grenades flying on the Northside."

Finn glances back at the wreckage, his gut twisting. He's been on the gang task force long enough to know that violence like this rarely stays contained.

Furman claps him on the shoulder. "You follow the gang lead. I'll dig into the Cruz connection. Maybe we'll meet in the middle."

Finn nods, though his mind is already racing. The threads are there-he just needs to untangle them.

He steps back under the police tape, pulling out his notepad. The morning sun glints off the shattered glass, and the distant wail of a siren echoes through the streets

Something big is brewing, and Finn knows this is only the beginning.

The golden morning sun glints off the calm ocean waves as Diane Sterling reclines in her luxurious leather chair, the warm light streaming through the floor-to-ceiling windows. She sips a mimosa leisurely, enjoying the serene view when her assistant, Edgar, strides into the room.

"Ma'am, the FBI has raided Global Strategies," Edgar announces, his voice steady.

Diane's eyes light up as she kicks her feet off the recliner and springs to her feet. Her excitement is evident, and a wicked grin spreads across her face.

"Perfect!" she exclaims, clapping her hands together. "It's all falling into place. That idiot won't know what hit him. No one outshines me!"

She strides across the room, grabbing her phone. Dialing quickly, she contacts CZL Holdings, the firm controlling the buying and selling of Global Strategies' stocks.

"This is Diane Sterling," she announces imperiously. "I want to make a large purchase of Global Strategies stock. As much as I can acquire."

The voice on the other end remains professional but firm. "Ms. Sterling, we'll need to vet and approve you first before proceeding with such a transaction."

Diane's face flushes with anger. "Vet me? I'm Diane Sterling!" she hisses, but the call ends before she can argue further.

She tosses her phone onto the table, the frustration boiling over. "Incompetent fools!" she mutters under her breath. Her grand plan—

to tank the stock value through scandal and buy it out—was now facing an unexpected hurdle.

She picks up her phone again and dials another number, one she knows will answer immediately.

"White Consulting, Stanley White speaking," comes the smooth voice on the other end.

"It's Diane, Mr. White. Did you hear the news?" she chirps, trying to mask her frustration.

"What news?" Stanley asks, his tone cautious.

"The Feds just raided Global Strategies!" Diane gushes, her voice brimming with excitement.

Before she can elaborate, Stanley cuts her off sharply. "Not on the phone. Meet me in an hour at the Sea Porch and Cabana Beach Club. Bring details."

The line goes dead before Diane can respond.

The sound of waves crashing against the shore is faint as Diane sits at a secluded table tucked away from prying eyes. The breeze ruffles her silk blouse as she taps her manicured nails on the table, waiting for Stanley.

Stanley arrives, dressed in a crisp linen suit, his expression dark as he sits across from her.

"What happened?" he asks without preamble.

Diane leans in, a giddy smile on her face as she begins to explain. "It worked! The information you gave me about the asset movements was solid. The FBI raided Global Strategies this morning!"

Stanley's expression remains stoic. "Any arrests? Media coverage? Anything concrete?"

Diane falters, her smile fading. "Well, no... not yet. I don't know."

Stanley's disappointment is evident as he leans back in his chair. "You don't know?" he repeats, his voice tinged with irritation. "This isn't a game, Diane. Scandals need substance to stick. Call me when you have something real."

Without waiting for her response, Stanley stands and walks away, leaving Diane sitting alone, her confidence shaken.

She stares blankly at the table, the clink of glasses and distant laughter from other patrons feeling miles away. For the first time, she feels out of her depth. The plan she had so meticulously crafted now seemed fragile, teetering on the brink of collapse.

"What now?" she whispers to herself, her fingers tightening around her glass as the morning sun continues to shine mockingly over the beach.

Brandon Corvin leans back in his sleek leather chair, the Miami skyline visible through the massive floor-to-ceiling windows behind him. The phone on his desk rings, followed almost simultaneously by the buzzing of his personal phone in his pocket.

With a sigh, he answers the desk phone. "Yes?" he says sharply into the speaker.

His assistant's voice is steady but urgent. "Mr. Corvin, you have a call from Agent Lane Gensler of the SEC. Should I put them through?"

Brandon's heart races. The SEC? Why now? His mind churns through potential reasons as his personal phone vibrates again in his pocket.

"No," he says finally, masking his unease. "Have them set an appointment. I'm not available right now." He ends the call abruptly and pulls out his personal phone, glancing at the screen.

A text from Tasha reads: Call me back.

He presses the call button, barely letting her phone finish the first ring, she answers.

"What's wrong?" he asks curtly, sensing the panic in the silence that follows.

Her words come in a frantic rush: "Brandon, the FBI raided Global Strategies this morning—there's talk of a shooting, a kidnapping, murder, and they're saying something about embezzlement! They took everything—records, computers, the works. It's bad, Brandon, really bad."

"Shut the fuck up," Brandon snaps, cutting her off. His voice is cold, commanding. "Too much talking, Tasha. Calm down. Are you at home?"

"Yes, but—"

"Stop," he interrupts. "Fly here tonight."

"I can't," she replies, her voice trembling. "I was directed to stay in the city. They told me not to leave."

Brandon clenches his jaw, pacing behind his desk. "Is your new spot ready yet?"

"Yes," she answers hesitantly.

"Good," he says, his tone now measured and icy. "Keep your fucking mouth shut. I'll see you in the morning." Without waiting for her reply, he hangs up.

Brandon's sleek black SUV tears up I-95 North as he grips the wheel, his knuckles white. His thoughts are a chaotic swirl of half-formed plans and worst-case scenarios.

"Damn it," he mutters, replaying Tasha's panicked words in his head. FBI. Kidnapping. Murder. Embezzlement. The pieces didn't add up. What had gone wrong?

As he nears Jacksonville, Brandon's mind sharpens, shifting into strategy mode. By the time he reaches Tasha's condo, he's ready to take control.

Tasha opens the door the moment Brandon knocks, her face pale and tear-streaked. She's still wearing the same designer blouse and skirt she'd worn during the raid, now wrinkled and stained with sweat.

"You took your time," she says, her voice breaking.

"Calm down," Brandon says, brushing past her into the dimly lit condo. He glances around, taking in the scattered papers and empty wine glass on the counter. "Tell me exactly what happened."

Tasha's hands shake as she begins to speak, her words spilling out in a torrent. "They came with a warrant—demanded everything.

Computers, files, phones. They questioned me about the asset transfers, the board firing, the shootings, and Robert's disappearance. Brandon, they think we're behind everything!" Her voice cracks as she adds, "I'm scared. They're going to find something—something that leads back to us!"

Brandon grabs her by the shoulders, forcing her to look at him. "Stop. Panicking. Right. Now," he says slowly, enunciating each word.

Tasha's lip quivers, but she nods, biting back her sobs.

"We've been careful," he says, his voice softening slightly. "Everything we've done has been through intermediaries. Nothing ties us directly to any of this. You didn't say anything stupid to them, did you?"

"No," she whispers, shaking her head.

"Good," he says, releasing her shoulders. "Now, sit down. We need to figure this out."

The two sit at the dining table, papers and laptops spread before them. The clock ticks past midnight as they piece together their cover story.

"Mob-Lee," Brandon says, scribbling on a notepad. "He's perfect. He's already connected to this mess through Robert and Vance. He looks capable of pulling off something like this."

Tasha's brow furrows. "But he doesn't have any motive—"

"Think," Brandon interrupts. "He was engaged to you, right? That's motive. Jealousy, resentment. We leak that he was furious about the breakup, and when Robert and Vance made moves that indirectly affected you, he snapped."

Tasha hesitates. "You think they'll buy it?"

"They'll have to," Brandon replies. "The FBI loves a clean narrative. We just need to plant the seeds."

"But what if they dig deeper?" she asks, her voice rising again.

Brandon slams his hand on the table, silencing her. "They won't. Not if we stay calm and stick to the story. The minute you start acting guilty, they'll pounce. So stop second-guessing me, Tasha. Do you trust me or not?"

She nods reluctantly. "I do."

"Good," Brandon says, leaning back in his chair. "Then let's finish this plan. By morning, we'll have everything in place."

As the first light of dawn creeps through the windows, Tasha and Brandon sit in silence, their makeshift cover story ready to deploy. But unease lingers in the air, a silent reminder that their web of lies is as fragile as the dawn breaking around them.

Aura-Lee sits in front of her glowing monitor in her private study, her fingers flying over the keyboard. A chat window pops up, and she quickly types a message:
Aura-Lee: Hey, where you at?

Moments later, her phone buzzes with a reply.
Mob-Lee: Staying low-key.

Aura-Lee rolls her eyes and types back immediately.
Aura-Lee: Call me.

Her phone vibrates almost instantly, and she answers without hesitation.

"Did you hear?" Aura-Lee asks.

Mob-Lee's voice is steady but guarded. "Yeah. They raided the headquarters."

Aura-Lee exhales sharply. "Not that. You remember Diane Sterling from the gala?"

Mob-Lee pauses, then replies, "Yeah."

"Well," Aura-Lee says, leaning forward, "that hoe called CZL Holdings today. Wanna know why?"

"Uh, duh," Mob-Lee says, a smirk audible in his tone.

"She wanted to buy as much Global Strategies stock as possible," Aura-Lee says.

Mob-Lee's tone shifts to serious. "Why would she want to do that?"

"I don't know," Aura-Lee says, frowning. "But the timing's too perfect. Right after the raid? Think it's connected?"

Mob-Lee's mind races. He doesn't reply immediately, processing the information.

Aura-Lee breaks the silence. "I'm going to look into her. This doesn't feel like a coincidence."

"Do that," Mob-Lee says.

They exchange a few more theories before ending the call.

Mob-Lee sits alone in the dimly lit command center of Discovery Dive Center, a covert facility he's been quietly setting up as his base. The room is filled with state-of-the-art tech—monitors, encrypted servers, and surveillance tools.

He leans back in his chair, staring at the folder on the desk before him. It's thick with documents—family secrets handed to him just before Robert's death.

"Diane Sterling," he mutters to himself, flipping through the files. "Why the hell would she want Global Strategies stock right after the raid? What's her angle?"

His mind spins through possibilities. Is she trying to profit off the chaos? Or is she cleaning up loose ends?

He pauses on a photo of Diane at the gala, her polished smile hiding sharp intent. Aura-Lee's right. This isn't a coincidence. But what's her connection to the raid? And who's feeding her information?

His gaze shifts to a document with a cryptic note "The connection runs deeper than it looks."

Mob-Lee exhales sharply. "Deeper than it looks," he repeats,

drumming his fingers on the desk. His mind shifts back to Diane. Is she a pawn, or is she playing the game at a higher level than we thought?

He logs into his secure server, pulling up a dossier on Diane. As he scrolls through her public achievements and hidden dealings, he can't shake the feeling that she's just one piece of a much larger puzzle.

"Alright, Sterling," he mutters, "let's see what you're really hiding."

Back at the Mitchell Estate, Aura-Lee sits in her lavish study, her laptop glowing with information about Diane Sterling. She picks up the phone and dials Logan Livingston.

Logan enters the room a few minutes later, dressed in his usual tailored suit, his expression unreadable.

"You called?" Logan says, standing by the door.

Aura-Lee gestures for him to sit. "Close the door and take a seat. I need your help."

Logan sits across from her, his sharp eyes scanning her face. "What's the situation?"

"It's Diane Sterling," Aura-Lee begins. "She called CZL Holdings today, trying to buy up Global Strategies stock—right after the raid."

Logan raises an eyebrow. "Interesting. What's her motive?"

"That's what I want to figure out," Aura-Lee says, leaning forward. "I'm already digging into her background, but I need you to focus on BFTB."

Logan frowns. "Possible connection?"

"I don't think so" Aura-Lee says. "I just can't watch Diane and BFTB at the same time."

Logan nods, his mind already working. "Understood. Anything else?"

Logan hesitates for a moment, then adds, "Be careful, Aura-Lee. Diane might not be just some socialite. If she's involved, she'll have contingencies. If Diane Sterling is as dangerous as we think she is, we can't afford any mistakes."
"

Aura-Lee smirks. "You know me. I'm always careful."

Aura-Lee then gives him a sharp look.

Logan rises, straightening his jacket. "I'll keep you updated."

As he leaves, Aura-Lee leans back in her chair, her mind racing. Diane Sterling was playing a dangerous game, and Aura-Lee was determined to figure out the rules before it was too late.

Chapter 11

Mob-Lee sits at the helm of his newly dubbed "Mob Manor," the heart of his secret command center at Discovery Dive Center. The room hums with activity as monitors flicker, displaying streams of data. Stacks of folders surround him, each filled with the Mitchell family's secrets. A separate file sits open on the desk: Diane Sterling.

Mob-Lee leans back, scrolling through her profile. "To be such a potential threat, she's quite unremarkable," he mutters. "Nothing screams 'mastermind' here." He shakes his head, dismissing the thought. "Aura-Lee says she'll handle Diane."

Turning his focus to another set of profiles built by Logan, he pulls up information on BFTB. He scans through names, pausing to smirk at the four from Monaco, now marked as Deceased.

His attention shifts to a particular profile: Shawn "BabyBoy" Hammond. The name has been on his radar for days. Mob-Lee taps the screen lightly. "You're next," he says under his breath, a hint of a smirk playing on his lips.

He scribbles some notes, rips the page from his notebook, folds it, and tucks it into the pocket of his jacket draped over the chair.

The sharp buzz of his phone pulls him from his thoughts. It's a text from Aura-Lee:

Aura-Lee: Feds want us to meet tomorrow at the headquarters to discuss the raid.

Mob-Lee quickly replies:
Mob-Lee: OK, we'll go at 1 PM. Might as well get something to eat before.

He adds several laughing emojis to lighten the mood, though his mind is anything but calm.

Turning back to his screen, Mob-Lee dives into the relationship between Black Sky Group and Global Strategies. His eyes narrow as he notices random asset movements between the two entities. It's subtle—almost too subtle—but there's a pattern.

Assets would transfer from Black Sky Group to Global Strategies, only to disappear shortly after.

"Hidden in plain sight," Mob-Lee mutters, his brain working overtime to piece it together.

A sudden memory jolts him back in time.

A year earlier, Mob-Lee and Tasha sat across from each other at a cozy dinner spot. She was radiant, her smile wide as she gushed over her new job.

"Tasha Nicole Sinclair," she said dramatically, raising her wine glass. "Vice President of Operations at Global Strategies."

Mob-Lee smiled warmly. "I'm proud of you, Tash. I knew you could do it."

The memory fades, and Mob-Lee stares blankly at the screen. "Tasha," he says aloud, his voice barely a whisper.

His heart skips a beat as the pieces begin to fall into place. Then, the weight of the realization hits him like a ton of bricks.

"She set us up," he thinks, his stomach churning.

He turns back to his computer, furiously typing. Every keystroke unravels another layer of Tasha's deception—her connections, her motivations, and how deeply she's intertwined in this web of lies.

"She used me. Used us all," he mutters, his jaw tightening.

As the hours tick by, Mob-Lee's resolve hardens. He isn't just searching for answers anymore—he's planning his next move. He has to save his company, his family's reputation, and, most importantly, himself.

He leans back in his chair, staring at Tasha's name on the screen. "You picked the wrong one to betray," he whispers, his eyes blazing with determination.

Tasha sits in the Global Strategies, fluorescent-lit conference room, her eyes red from lack of sleep. Across the table are Agent Taylor and Agent Alvarez, their pens poised over notebooks, recording every word she says.

"I'm telling you," Tasha insists, her voice trembling just enough to seem sincere. "Mob-Lee authorized those asset movements. He's been angry for years, and this whole feud with Robert and Vance was bound to explode."

She takes a breath, feigning emotional turmoil. "He blamed them for everything, even for us breaking up. He was obsessed with control, with proving he was better than them."

Agent Taylor leans forward, nodding sympathetically. "So you're saying Mob-Lee orchestrated all of this—out of jealousy and rage?"

Tasha nods solemnly. "Exactly. He has a temper. I thought I could help him, but... I couldn't."

Agent Alvarez, more reserved, studies her carefully. "And the kidnapping? The shooting? You're saying he could've planned all of that?"

Tasha swallows hard, her hands clasped tightly in her lap. "I can't prove it, but... it's possible. You don't know him like I do."

The agents exchange a glance, Alvarez's expression skeptical, but Taylor seems convinced.

At exactly 1 PM, the door to the conference room swings open. Aura-Lee and Mob-Lee stride in confidently, followed by a sharply dressed legal counsel carrying a leather-bound briefcase.

Before anyone can speak, the attorney hands Agent Alvarez a stack of documents. "This should provide some much-needed clarity," the lawyer says curtly.

Agent Taylor, emboldened by Tasha's story, wastes no time. "We've already got plenty of clarity," she says sharply, flipping through her notes. "Mr. Mitchell set up his ex to take the fall for things he was doing out jealousy—"

Aura-Lee interrupts with a sharp laugh. "Mob-Lee, you dated this bubblehead-ass bitch? Eww, bruh."

Tasha looks at Aura-Lee angrily.

Mob-Lee chuckles, shaking his head. "And this is exactly why I didn't say anything."

Agent Taylor frowns, trying to regain control of the conversation. She pushes a stack of documents across the table. "These signatures—your signatures—authorize the transfer of assets. Care to explain?"

Before Mob-Lee can respond, Agent Alvarez, flipping through the newly provided documents, holds up a hand. "Hold on, Taylor. He's got something here that challenges her whole story."

Mob-Lee leans forward, his tone calm but firm. "We didn't take control of Global Strategies until October 2nd. The ceremony was just for show—we didn't sign anything official that night. We didn't even have access to the systems or authority to make decisions before then. All of that was still under the previous administration. "

He gestures to the documents. "Look at the dates. October 1st. We were taking care of Vance and trying to find Robert. And as you can see here—" he points to the new evidence Alvarez is examining, "—the actual asset movements started happening long before I even knew I'd inherit Global Strategies."

Agent Taylor's confidence wavers. She looks to Tasha. "You said he authorized this. How do you explain these discrepancies?"

Tasha, her face pale, stammers. "I... I don't know. Maybe he found a way to—"

Agent Alvarez cuts her off, holding up another document. "Ms. Sinclair, your login credentials are all over this. Every single transfer was authorized under your account, using your unique access key. The timestamps don't lie."

Tasha's breath hitches. Tears well up in her eyes as she realizes the walls are closing in.

"Ms. Sinclair," Alvarez says, standing, "you're under arrest for embezzlement, conspiracy to defraud, and obstruction of justice."

As Agent Alvarez begins to read her rights, Tasha snaps. Tears stream down her face as she looks at Mob-Lee, pleading.

"Mob-Lee, please!" she cries. "You loved me! Why couldn't you be the man you are now when we were together? I did this for us!"

Mob-Lee's expression remains cold. "I did love you," he says quietly. "But you just had to fuck around and find out."

Tasha screams his name as she's escorted out of the room, her cries echoing down the hallway.

Aura-Lee, leaning against the table, watches the scene unfold with disgust. She turns to Mob-Lee, shaking her head. "Eww, bruh. Just... eww."

Mob-Lee smirks. "Lesson learned."

Aura-Lee rolls her eyes. "Let's hope so."

The siblings leave the room, their lawyer in tow, ready to focus on the next challenge.

Agents Taylor and Alvarez sit in disbelief

Mob-Lee and Aura-Lee step out of the Global Strategies headquarters, the weight of the morning's confrontation finally lifting from their shoulders. The cool breeze hits them, and both exchange a glance of mutual understanding.

"That went better than expected," Aura-Lee says, tucking a stray strand of hair behind her ear.

"Yeah, but I'm still pissed it got this far," Mob-Lee replies, his tone lighter now.

"See you later, bruh," she says, pulling out her phone to call her driver.

"Later, sis," Mob-Lee responds with a nod, already dialing Destiny's number.

As Mob-Lee walks to his car, Destiny answers on the second ring. "Mob-Lee, what's the word?"

"All good on our end. The FBI's off the company for now. They're focused on finding out who else was involved," he explains.

Destiny exhales audibly. "Thank God. You and Aura-Lee worked miracles."

Mob-Lee smirks. "It's what we do."

"Hey," she says after a pause, her tone softening. "You free to grab a quick bite? I've been craving Blue Boys Diner since my brother and I went there the other day."

He glances at his watch. "You buying?"

She laughs. "Of course."

"Then I'm on my way," Mob-Lee replies, starting the car.

Thirty minutes later, Mob-Lee and Destiny sit across from each other in a corner booth at Blue Boys Diner. The aroma of fresh coffee and grilled burgers fills the air.

Destiny dives into her meal, savoring each bite. Mob-Lee, arms crossed, watches her with amusement.

"Didn't realize you loved diner food this much," he teases.

Destiny wipes her mouth with a napkin, grinning. "Sometimes, a girl just needs greasy comfort food."

"Fair enough." He leans back in the booth. "So, the FBI's pivoting. Tasha being the lead suspect and she out of the picture, their focus is on tracing the other players. We're in the clear for now, but we need to stay ahead."

Destiny nods, relieved. "Good. That means we can get back to business—and maybe breathe a little easier."

She sets down her fork and looks at him thoughtfully. "Speaking of business, would you be willing to join me at a fundraiser in New York City this weekend? It's a big networking opportunity."

Mob-Lee arches an eyebrow. "What's the dress code?"

Destiny grins. "Remember that navy-blue set we wore to the gala? Nobody outside the party saw it, so we could reuse it. Matching power moves, you know?"

He chuckles. "You've got a plan for everything, don't you?"

"Of course."

"Count me in," he says with a smile. "I've got a few loose ends to tie up in town, but we can leave tomorrow morning."

"Perfect," Destiny replies, finishing her plate.

Outside the diner, Mob-Lee walks Destiny to her sleek, white car. The late afternoon sun glints off the vehicle as they linger by the door.

"Thanks for lunch," Mob-Lee says, leaning against the car.

"Thanks for keeping the company afloat," she counters, smirking.

They share a brief hug, lingering just long enough to feel the unspoken tension between them.

"I'll call you later to sort out the details," she says, sliding into the driver's seat.

"Sounds good," Mob-Lee replies, stepping back as she starts the engine.

As she drives off, Mob-Lee watches her go, a faint smile on his face.

Destiny is still smiling as she merges onto the highway when her phone buzzes. She answers after checking the caller ID.

"Hey, I was just thinking about you," she says warmly.

On the other end, Kevin, her brother, sounds less cheerful. "Yeah, I just saw you leaving Blue Boys Diner. Who was old boy you were all hugged up on?"

Destiny laughs, brushing off his tone. "Relax, Kevin. That's just a business associate... for now," she adds with a playful giggle.

"Don't make me have to hurt somebody," Kevin says, only half-joking.

"I love you, Kevin," she replies. "If it turns into something, you'll be the first to know, okay?"

He sighs. "Alright. Just know I'll hurt a motherf—"

"Bye, Kevin," she interrupts, laughing as she ends the call.

Kevin tosses his phone onto the passenger seat, his unease lingering. There's something about that guy... something familiar he just can't shake.

Kevin, still thinking about the man hugging Destiny, sits at a booth in Blue Boys Diner, his food in a brown paper bag on the table. He drums his fingers against the counter, replaying the scene in his head.

"Who drives a Bentley to Blue Boys?" he mutters to himself. The familiarity of the man's silhouette bothers him, but he can't place it. His phone buzzes, pulling him out of his thoughts.

Text from BabyBoy: "I'm at the spot whenever you're ready."

Kevin stands, tossing a few bills on the table, and heads for the door.

A dark room with mismatched furniture. Guns, ammunition, and cash are scattered across the table.

Kevin pushes open the door, the smell of gunpowder and stale air hitting him. BabyBoy is seated, grinning as he gestures to the arsenal of weapons sprawled out.

BabyBoy: "You see this, Top? This right here is what's gonna make them regret ever breathin'. Got everything from Glocks to ARs. Even got a few toys from overseas."

TopBoy: [Examining the weapons] "This is heavy. You been workin', huh?"

BabyBoy: "Ain't had a choice. Four of ours, gone, Top. That ain't sittin' right with me."

Kevin grips one of the guns, the cold metal steadying his rage.

TopBoy: "They ain't just gone. They got snatched from us. That's our blood, our money, our name in the streets. This feels like some Coastline bullshit.

BabyBoy: "So what's the move, then? We takin' it to their door or hittin' 'em where it hurts?"

TopBoy: "Both. We bleed 'em dry, then we burn what's left. I want their stash houses, their corners, their connections. If they got alliances, we sever 'em. I want their whole operation crumblin' before they even know what hit 'em."

BabyBoy: "You got somethin' specific in mind?"

TopBoy: "We start small. Recon their spots, see where they're weak. Hit 'em when they least expect it. I want their soldiers shook, their bosses paranoid, and their bankrolls empty. But we keep it quiet—no mess, no loose ends. If anyone talks, we clean it up."

BabyBoy nods, a wicked grin spreading across his face. "I'm wit' it. Let's make it hurt."

A loud knock echoes through the house. Kevin motions for BabyBoy to stash the weapons.

TopBoy: "Hide all this shit, now."

BabyBoy quickly gathers the guns, hiding them under a couch and in secret compartments. Kevin opens the door to see Detective Finn standing there in plain clothes.

Detective Finn: "What's up, Kevin? Mind if I come in for a minute?"

Kevin steps aside, reluctantly letting him in.

Detective Finn: [Looking around] "Sorry for your loss. Heard about what happened. Four of your guys, right?"

TopBoy: "Yeah. You got any leads, or you just here to waste my time?"

Detective Finn: "I'm just askin' questions. You got any idea who might've done this?"

TopBoy: "If I did, it wouldn't be your issue."

Finn sighs, crossing his arms. "Look, Kevin, I get it. You're mad. You want payback. But revenge? That's a slippery slope. You start this war, it's gonna end bad—for everybody."

Kevin's jaw tightens, his eyes blazing with fury. "You think you're droppin' wisdom? Get the fuck outta my house and do your fuckin' job."

Finn hesitates, then nods. "Just think about what I said. Give me a call before you do anything stupid."

He leaves, and Kevin slams the door behind him.

The trap house is alive with tension. Kevin, aka TopBoy, stands at the center of the dimly lit room. The smell of weed lingers in the air, mingling with the sharp tang of gun oil from the arsenal BabyBoy laid out earlier. Surrounding him are the surviving members of BFTB, each holding drinks or weapons, their faces hardened with grief and anger.

Kevin takes a long pull from his blunt, the ember glowing bright in the shadowed room. He exhales slowly, letting the smoke curl around him like a shroud before slamming his fist on the table to command attention.

"Look around you!" Kevin's voice booms, cutting through the chatter and haze. "Look at who's left standing! We started this shit as a family, and now what? Four of our brothers are gone. Deceased. Murdered. They didn't just take soldiers from us—they took sons, fathers, and brothers. And what the fuck has the system done about it? Not a damn thing."

He points to the weapons BabyBoy brought in. "This right here? This is how we handle our business. The cops ain't gonna give us justice. They don't care about BFTB, they never did. So, we're gonna make them care. We're gonna make everybody care."

Kevin paces the room, his eyes locking with each member. "On the dead guys, we're spinnin' every damn day until every single one of these Coastline pussies feels what we feel right now. Pain. Loss. Rage."

He pauses, gripping the edge of the table as his voice drops into a deadly calm. "This ain't just about revenge. This is about respect. They thought they could cross us and walk away clean? Nah. We're putting a price on it—a million dollars cash to whoever brings me the heads of the ones responsible."

The room erupts in murmurs of shock and excitement. Kevin raises his hand to silence them.

"You heard me right. One. Million. Dollars. Dead or alive, I don't care how it gets done. Coastline's been a problem since my father's time.

He steps closer to the group, his voice rising again. "This ain't just a hit. This is war. From the coastline to the city, we're gonna make them feel our pain. And I don't want just shooters—I want strategists. Thinkers. Every corner of this city, I want it locked down.

Every ally they got? Burn that bridge. Every move they make? We're ten steps ahead."

He points to BabyBoy. "We got the tools. We got the manpower. Now we got the motivation. I want everybody locked in, focused. No loose lips, no weak links. We move as one, we strike as one, and we take everything back that they took from us."

Kevin leans back, his voice dropping into a deadly whisper that carries through the room. "When we're done, Coastline won't just regret crossing us—they'll wish they never existed."

This ain't just about hittin' back—it's about takin' over. Every corner, every dollar, every soldier they got? That's ours now. And if anyone else got a problem with it, they can get it too.

We're movin' smart, we're movin' fast, and we ain't stoppin' till the streets are ours. Coastline dies tonight. Who's wit' me?"

He raises his drink in the air. "For the fallen, for the family, and for the bag. Let's get to work."

The room erupts into cheers and war cries. Kevin steps down, his resolve solidified.

Kevin and BabyBoy huddle with a few key members, laying out their strategy. Each crew is assigned a specific task—staking out stash houses, intercepting supply routes, and identifying key players.

As the night deepens, Kevin looks out the window, his mind racing. He's ready for war, but a lingering thought gnaws at him: the man at the diner.

Who the hell was he?

Logan's Range Rover hummed along, the steady sound of tires on pavement cutting through the silence. Mob-Lee sat with his arms crossed, staring out of the passenger window, trying to wrap his mind around what he was about to walk into. He glanced at the sign as Logan pulled off onto a gravel road—Bert Maxwell Boat Ramp.

"Where we going, Logan?" Mob-Lee asked, raising an eyebrow.

Logan grinned like he was about to drop a huge secret. "Someone's dying to meet you."

They pulled up next to a sleek black Escalade, and Mob-Lee squinted through the windshield. The gravel crunched under Logan's tires as they parked, and before Mob-Lee could ask more questions, a gruff voice rang out, "Dutchie! Is this him?"

Logan smirked. "Yeah, this is Deacon's son."

A big, burly guy—wearing a leather jacket that screamed "I've been through some things"—stepped into view. His face was covered in a thick beard, but his eyes were as warm as a teddy bear's. He practically bounded over to them, slapping Logan on the back in an exaggerated, overly affectionate way

"Mob-Lee, my man!" Deuce called out, pulling Mob-Lee into an enthusiastic bear hug that completely caught him off guard.

Mob-Lee stiffened for a moment, but after a couple of awkward pats on Deuce's back, he reluctantly hugged back.

Logan chuckled at the exchange. "Mob-Lee, this is Deuce. Deuce, Mob-Lee Mitchell—Deacon's kid."

Deuce grinned so widely it looked like his face might split in two. "A grenade!?" he exclaimed, practically bouncing on his heels. "Reminds me of the time Deacon—"

Logan quickly cut in, giving Deuce a pointed look. "Don't, Deuce."

Deuce waved him off with a dramatic flourish. "What? You telling me this boy can throw a grenade in broad daylight and I can't tell him a story?"

Mob-Lee raised an eyebrow. "I want to hear the story," he said, his curiosity piqued.

Deuce leaned in like he was about to tell a ghost story. "Your dad shot an RPG at some of the Bottom Boys," he started, eyes lighting up as he leaned closer. "These punks had shot up the neighborhood, didn't realize it was just one big circle—one way in, one way out. So when they came back around, your pops is just sitting there in the middle of the street, in his boxers, like he's about to pray... holding an RPG." Deuce threw his head back, letting out a laugh. "Man, sent those boys straight to Jesus. The upper room!" he and Logan shouted in unison, cracking up.

Mob-Lee snorted, trying to hold it together. "Man, that's wild."

Deuce was now completely enamored with Mob-Lee's "grenade incident." "You know," Deuce began, leaning back with a dramatic flair, "you've really outdone your old man with that grenade throw. I mean, it's like—boom!—you're taking out the whole damn parking lot with one toss."

Logan rolled his eyes but couldn't help but chuckle. "A grenade's got a lot of power, man."

Deuce, still riding the grenade high, shot out a few random jokes about explosions. "You ever notice how a car explosion is like a really bad breakup? One minute, it's all 'I love you,' and the next, it's BOOM, nothing left but a trail of smoke and regret."

Mob-Lee chuckled. "Yeah, and the worst part? They never leave a note. Just... gone."

"Exactly!" Deuce howled. "Man, you got a future in this!"

Mob-Lee raised an eyebrow. "So, do you guys always just stand around talking about blowing things up?"

Deuce threw an arm around his shoulder. "You have to have fun with this stuff, Mob-Lee. You ever say anything cool before throwing a grenade?"

Mob-Lee smirked. "Well, I did say 'catch,' but that's just me keeping it simple."

Deuce immediately cracked up, then leaned in close like he was about to drop the greatest catchphrase of all time. "I always wanted to say something like, 'Time to take out the trash!'"

Logan groaned. "I swear, you guys are like two kids at a candy store."

The three of them stood there, riffing on grenade-related puns for what seemed like an eternity. Eventually, Deuce wiped a tear from his eye. "Man, you've got Deacon's fire in you, no doubt."

They took a breather before the conversation took a more serious turn. Deuce grinned, tapping Mob-Lee on the chest like they were sharing a big secret. "You know, Mob-Lee, being a part of Coastline isn't just about blowing things up—it's about loyalty, family. Your dad ran things like a king. A lot of people respected him."

Mob-Lee nodded, trying to process it all. "So, what does that mean for me now?"

Deuce leaned in, eyes glinting. "It means you've got a whole new world ahead of you. Coastline's got your back, kid. And trust me, if you ever need anything—anything—just holler." He paused, then grinned mischievously. "Oh, and we should show you the handshake. You know, for real. It's all about the gesture."

Logan gave Deuce a pointed look. "You're joking, right?"

Deuce raised an eyebrow, deadpan. "I'm not joking. This is serious."

With that, the three men shared a few more pleasantries, clapping each other on the back.

As they parted ways, Mob-Lee couldn't help but feel the weight of everything he'd just learned. Not only did he now know about his father's ties to the Coastline Mafia, but he had just made connections with men who were definitely on the darker side of things.

Logan and Mob-Lee got into the Range Rover, the air around them thick with thought. Mob-Lee turned to Logan. "So, what's next? What do we do with all this new information?"

Logan's face was focused, and Mob-Lee knew better than to push him. They had just scratched the surface, and something told him the deeper they went, the messier things would get. He couldn't shake the feeling that the more he learned about his legacy, the more insane it all seemed.

As they drove off, Mob-Lee pulled out his phone, staring at the screen. He quickly typed out a message to Destiny: Call you in a few so we can plan this trip. I need to get out of Duval for a while.

He hit send and leaned back in his seat, the weight of everything pressing down on him. He couldn't escape the feeling that, no matter where he went, the insanity was only just beginning.

Chapter 12: baecation

A Private jet sitting on the runway, interior lavishly decorated in muted tones of cream and gold. Mob-Lee and Destiny are seated across from each other on plush leather chairs.

Mob-Lee smirking as he sets his phone on airplane mode:
"Alright, phones off. No distractions this weekend."

Destiny doing the same:
"Deal. Just us, champagne, and the city that never sleeps."

They clink their champagne glasses, the sound of the engines humming in the background.

Destiny:
"Crazy how life works. I can't believe we went to the same middle school. I mean, what are the odds?"

Mob-Lee chuckling
"Yeah, small world. I was the skinny kid with glasses and a bad haircut. You wouldn't have noticed me."

Destiny (laughing):
"I doubt that. You probably stuck out with all those brains. Didn't you skip a grade?"

Mob-Lee (shrugging):
"Yeah, after middle school. Guess I missed my chance to hang out with the cool kids."

Destiny (playfully):
"You mean me?"

Mob-Lee:
"Obviously."

They laugh, sipping champagne as the jet climbs through the clouds, leaving Jacksonville behind.

Time: 2:31 PM. The jet touches down smoothly. Destiny glances at her watch and frowns slightly.

Destiny:
"It's 2:31. They said we'd land at 2:30. I hate when people can't stick to their word."

Mob-Lee (grinning):
"You're really gonna let one minute ruin the vibe?"

Destiny (sighing):
"Fine, fine. But I'm keeping an eye on the time from now on."

They descend the stairs to a waiting black car. The driver opens the door as Mob-Lee hands over their garment bags.

Driver:
"Welcome to New York. Aman's expecting you."

They cruise through the bustling city streets, taking in the sights and sounds before pulling up to the luxury hotel.

The Hotel lobby, opulent with towering ceilings, sleek marble floors, and a soft ambient glow. Mob-Lee approaches the reception desk. Destiny lingers nearby, admiring the décor.

Mob-Lee (to the receptionist, reading her name tag):
"Room for Mitchell."

Karen, the receptionist, gives him a once-over, her expression shifting to thinly veiled disdain. Mob-Lee's outfit—worn t-shirt, grey sweatpants, and house shoes—contrasts starkly with the hotel's upscale clientele.

Karen (forcing a polite tone):
"Are you sure you're in the right place? Rooms here start at thirty-two hundred dollars a night. You might want to try somewhere more…appropriate."

Mob-Lee (unbothered):
"Just check the name."

Karen (hesitant, crossing her arms):
"I don't think I need to. We don't usually accommodate…walk-ins like this."

Destiny steps forward, eyebrows raised.

Destiny:
"Is there a problem here?"

Mob-Lee (waving her off):
"No problem. She just hasn't typed in my name yet."

Karen (scoffing):
"I'm trying to save you some embarrassment. Why don't you try a Holiday Inn?"

Karen discreetly presses a button. Two security officers approach.

Security Officer 1:
"Is there an issue?"

Karen (pointing at Mob-Lee):
"This gentleman doesn't belong here and is causing a disturbance."

Mob-Lee (calmly):
"Disturbance? I just asked for my room."

Security Officer 2 (gruffly):
"Sir, we're gonna have to ask you to leave."

(Mob-Lee steps back, his expression hardening.)

Mob-Lee:
"Leave? Without my room keys? I don't think so."

The security officers move closer, but before they can act, the manager arrives, his demeanor polished and professional.

Manager (sternly to Karen):
"What's going on here?"

Karen:
"This man is loitering—"

Manager (interrupting, looking at Mob-Lee):
"Mr. Mitchell. My sincerest apologies for this misunderstanding. Your suite is ready, of course."

Karen's jaw drops as the manager turns to Destiny.

Manager:
"Ms. Knight, a pleasure to have you with us as well. Let me personally escort you to the presidential suite."

The manager glares at Karen.

Manager:
"We'll discuss this later."

Karen stammers, her face pale.

Karen:
"But I didn't know—"

Manager:
"No excuses. Apologize to Mr. Mitchell and Ms. Knight immediately."

Karen mumbles an apology. Mob-Lee smirks but doesn't respond. The manager hands them their keys and gestures for a porter to take their garment bags.

Fifth Avenue. Mob-Lee and Destiny stroll between luxury boutiques, their shopping bags multiplying by the minute. Mob-Lee continues to draw skeptical looks from staff.

Sales Associate (eyeing Mob-Lee):
"Are you sure you're in the right store?"

(Mob-Lee pulls out an exclusive blue metal bank card, handing it over. The associate's demeanor changes instantly.)

Sales Associate (beaming):
"Of course, sir. Would you like that gift-wrapped?"

Destiny (laughing as they leave the store):
"walking around in those debos is throwing these people off. Are you like a billionaire incognito."

Mob-Lee (grinning):
"Where's the fun in being obvious?"

They continue shopping, pausing at a rooftop bar for drinks and a breathtaking view of the city.

A high-end restaurant. Mob-Lee and Destiny enjoy a lavish dinner, their table adorned with gourmet dishes.

Destiny (sipping wine):
"This day has been...unexpected. From that receptionist to the shopping sprees. You sure know how to keep things interesting."

Mob-Lee (smirking):
"Wait until tomorrow. The fundraiser will be a whole new level of chaos."

They return to the hotel with their arms full of shopping bags. Mob-Lee tips the porter generously as they prepare for the next day's event.

The suite is bathed in soft, golden sunlight. Destiny stirs as the light filters through the curtains, while Mob-Lee is already awake, stretching by the window.

Mob-Lee (grinning):
"Rise and shine, Miss Swiss Engineering. Wouldn't want to be late for the genius convention."

Destiny groans and grabs a pillow, playfully tossing it at him.

Destiny (smirking):
"Fine, fine. Let me get ready. Don't rush me, Mr. Perfectly On Time."

Destiny heads into the bathroom, and 30 minutes later, she emerges looking effortlessly chic in a Chanel Athletics bodysuit. Mob-Lee, dressed in his all-black Nike Tech workout gear, looks her up and down.

Mob-Lee (raising an eyebrow):
"When did Chanel start making workout clothes?"

Destiny (with a sly smile):
"Always ahead of the curve. You should know that by now."

They share a laugh as they grab their things and head out.

The elevator descends smoothly to the lobby. Destiny adjusts her hair in the mirrored walls while Mob-Lee leans against the side, hands in his pockets.

Destiny (softly):
"Thanks for coming today. I know it's not your usual scene."

Mob-Lee (smirking):
"Yeah, I'm more of a punching bags and code-breaking kinda guy, but for you? I'll make an exception."

Destiny smiles and shakes her head.

Mob-Lee:
"Real talk, though—what's this fundraiser about?"

Destiny:
"It's for underprivileged youth who want to pursue STEM careers. We're giving them a glimpse of what's possible, showing them they can achieve anything."

Mob-Lee (nodding thoughtfully):
"Oh, so we're hyping up the smart-smart Black kids. Love that."

Destiny laughs, and the elevator dings as they step out into the lively New York morning.

A sectioned-off area in Central Park is bustling with volunteers setting up tents, tables, and activity stations. Mob-Lee and Destiny arrive right on time.

Destiny (surveying the scene):

"Everything looks perfect. Let's make this day unforgettable for them."

Mob-Lee jumps in to help, moving tables, carrying supplies, and chatting with volunteers. His natural charisma makes an impression on everyone around him.

Volunteer (smiling):
"Thanks for lending a hand, Mr. Mitchell. You're a natural at this."

Mob-Lee (grinning):
"Just trying to keep up with the boss over here."

Destiny shakes her head but can't hide her smile as they work side by side, setting up for the day.

Families and kids arrive, filling the park with energy and laughter. The activity stations are alive with excitement as kids move from one game to the next.

1. Obstacle Course:

Kids navigate tunnels, climb walls, and balance on beams, learning about physics through motion. Mob-Lee demonstrates, making it look effortless.

Mob-Lee (to a group of wide-eyed kids):
"Physics is simple—gravity just wants you to stay down. We don't listen to gravity."

The kids laugh and cheer as he flips off a balance beam.

2. STEM-Themed Scavenger Hunt:

Teams search for hidden items like toy robots, building blocks, and circuit pieces, following clues tied to STEM concepts.

Destiny:
"Who can tell me how many planets are in our solar system? First correct answer gets a clue!"

Kids excitedly shout answers, racing to find the next clue.

3. Water Balloon Toss:

Pairs toss balloons back and forth, practicing precision and teamwork. Mob-Lee joins in, dramatically "dodging" balloons to make the kids laugh.

4. Freeze Tag with a Twist:

To unfreeze, kids answer STEM trivia questions. Mob-Lee and Destiny each lead a team, playfully trying to outsmart each other.

Mob-Lee:
"Don't let Team Destiny fool you—they're good at trivia, but we've got the speed."

Destiny laughs as her team unfreezes another player.

5. Kickball Finale:

The highlight of the day. Families gather around to watch as Mob-Lee and Destiny captain opposing teams.

The game is intense and full of laughter. Mob-Lee's team takes an early lead, but Destiny's team rallies back. In the final play, Mob-Lee dramatically slides into home base, scoring the winning point.

Destiny (grinning despite herself):
"Alright, you win this time. But only because my team let you."

Mob-Lee (mock bowing):

"All hail the kickball champ."

The kids swarm him, cheering and laughing, while Destiny watches from the sidelines, smiling warmly. She can't help but admire the way Mob-Lee connects with the children, his playful nature masking a deeper care for their happiness.

The suite is calm and quiet after the bustling day. Destiny sits at the vanity, applying light makeup in preparation for the fundraiser ball. Mob-Lee emerges from the bathroom, freshly showered and adjusting his tie.

Destiny (glancing at him in the mirror):
"You clean up well, Mr. Mitchell."

Mob-Lee (smirking):
"Only because I've got an image to uphold. Don't want to embarrass you in front of all your fancy friends."

Destiny smiles, but there's a softness in her gaze. The day's events replay in her mind—the way Mob-Lee made the kids laugh, how he inspired them, and the effortless way he made everyone feel seen and valued.

Destiny (after a pause):
"You were incredible today. The kids adored you. I don't think I've ever seen anyone like you."

Mob-Lee, caught off guard, looks at her for a moment before his usual playful smirk returns.

Mob-Lee:
"Careful, Destiny. Keep talking like that, and I might think you actually like me."

Destiny laughs softly but doesn't deny it. There's a new tension in the air—one filled with unspoken feelings—as they finish getting ready and prepare to head out to the fundraiser ball.

A luxurious ballroom hosted by "Future Horizons Initiative," a nonprofit organization dedicated to advancing STEM education for underprivileged youth. Crystal chandeliers illuminate the room, casting golden light on the elegantly dressed attendees. A live string quartet plays soft music as servers glide through the crowd with champagne flutes.

Mob-Lee and Destiny enter together. Destiny, glowing in a sapphire gown, draws admiring glances, while Mob-Lee, in a perfectly tailored tuxedo, moves confidently at her side. Their entrance feels like a scene from a movie.

Mob-Lee (leaning in as they walk):
"So, what's the goal for tonight?"

Destiny (sighing):
"Officially, we're aiming for one million. But if we really want to meet the program's needs, we need closer to five."

Mob-Lee nods thoughtfully, his expression unreadable.

Destiny (spotting a group of board members):
"Excuse me for a moment. Duty calls."

Mob-Lee (with a smirk):
"Go save the world, Miss Swiss Engineering."

As Destiny moves to join the board members, Mob-Lee scans the room, his sharp eyes taking everything in. He spots the discreet donation box near the stage. Walking over casually, he pulls out his checkbook, writes a check, folds it, and slips it into the box without hesitation.

Destiny returns to Mob-Lee, now waiting for her near the bar with two glasses of champagne in hand. The warm glow of the room enhances the elegance of the evening.

Mob-Lee (offering her a glass):
"Thought you could use a drink after all that schmoozing."

Destiny (laughing as she takes the glass):
"You're not wrong. Thank you."

They clink glasses and sip, sharing a moment of quiet camaraderie. The music shifts to a slow, romantic tune.

Destiny (setting her glass down):
"Dance with me?"

Mob-Lee (raising an eyebrow):
"Not really my thing."

Destiny (smirking):
"Consider it part of your civic duty tonight."

She pulls him toward the dance floor. He relents, placing a hand on her waist as they join the other couples. They begin to sway, their movements growing more natural as the song progresses.

The dance floor glimmers under soft lights, the music enveloping them. Mob-Lee and Destiny move in perfect sync, their eyes locked.

Destiny (softly):
"You're full of surprises, you know that?"

Mob-Lee (with a smirk):
"Good surprises or bad?"

Destiny:
"Still deciding."

They fall silent as the music crescendos. Destiny rests her head on Mob-Lee's shoulder, and he tightens his hold on her waist. The world around them fades—no noise, no crowd, just the two of them. Time feels suspended until the song ends. They pull apart slightly, their faces inches apart, the intensity of the moment lingering between them.

Toward the end of the evening, the hostess steps onto the stage, beaming as she holds the donation box.

Hostess:
"Thank you all for your incredible generosity tonight. Let's see how much we've raised for Future Horizons Initiative!"

She begins announcing amounts as the total climbs steadily to $750,000. The crowd applauds enthusiastically.

Hostess (reaching into the box for the final check):
"And now, our last donation…"

Her voice falters, and her eyes widen as she reads the amount.

Hostess (excitedly):
"We did it! With this final donation of ten million dollars, we've surpassed our goal!"

The room erupts into cheers and applause, but the hostess isn't done. She looks back at the check.

Hostess:
"A special thank you to… Mob-Lee Mitchell."

The crowd turns to look at Mob-Lee, who raises his glass slightly, unfazed. Destiny stares at him, her mouth slightly open in shock.

In the back of a sleek black car on the way back to the hotel, Destiny can't contain her curiosity any longer.

Destiny:
"So… how rich are you?"

Mob-Lee chuckles, shaking his head.

Mob-Lee:
"Rich? Nah, I'm just… comfortable."

Destiny gives him a skeptical look.

Destiny:
"Comfortable doesn't explain ten million dollars like it's nothing."

Mob-Lee shrugs, clearly trying to downplay the moment. Destiny smirks.

Destiny:
"Well, I'm rich. But I'm trying to be wealthy."

She flicks an imaginary speck off her shoulder, making Mob-Lee laugh.

Mob-Lee:
"And what's wealthy?"

Destiny (grinning):
"One billion. Minimum."

Mob-Lee laughs, though there's a flicker of discomfort in his expression. They fall into a companionable silence as the car pulls up to their hotel. Inside, they step into the elevator.

Destiny, slightly tipsy, stumbles, and Mob-Lee catches her by the waist.

Their eyes meet, the chemistry between them undeniable. Slowly, Destiny leans in, and Mob-Lee closes the gap. Their lips meet in a passionate kiss, the elevator's soft chime signaling their ascent to the presidential suite.

the elevator doors close.

As the elevator doors glide open to the presidential suite, Mob-Lee and Destiny are lost in a passionate kiss, tearing each other's clothes off as the exit the elevator. Falling on to the couch hands moving up and down each other's body searching for skin.

Mob-Lee pauses, his expression gentle but searching. "Are you sure about this?" he asks quietly.

Destiny smiles, her voice steady. "I fully consent to everything that happens tonight. I trust you."

With that being said Mob-Lee finds the edge of Destiny's panties. Sliding them down. He's face first with his head between her thighs. She screams in ecstasy. Thighs trembling, hands slowly caressing the top of Mob-Lee's head. Using his tongue and fingers systematically. 5 minutes later Mob-Lee comes up for air. His face soaked. Juices dripping from his goatee.

Destiny kisses him deeply. Tongue moving around his face enjoying the taste of herself.

She grabs Mob-Lee pushing him up against the wall. She Unfastened his belt. Sliding her hand in his pants. She lowers to a squatting position as she places him in her mouth. Slow sensual movements. Then more enthusiastic slob filled motions. Alternating hands. Slapping him across her tongue repeatedly maintaining eye contact.

Mob-Lee lifts her to her full height kissing again.

Destiny suggests going on the balcony. He slips on a condom as he slips out of his pants.
Outside, the cool night air contrasts with the warmth between them. They lean against the railing, gazing at the glittering skyline. "It's beautiful," Destiny murmurs, her voice soft.

Mob-Lee glances at her, his gaze filled with sincerity. "Not as beautiful as this moment."

He bends her over the edge of the balcony while gripping a hand full of her hair. the other hand firm around her neck with just the right amount of pressure. Moans fill the night air.

Sitting on a well positioned chair Destiny straddles Mob-Lee. A slow purposeful bounce soon becomes more like a rodeo show.

The mood becomes playful as they retreat inside, taking their time to savor every second. Destiny now on her back on the bed she scratches deeply in to Mob-Lee's back. Their chocolate skin blending beautiful and he firmly grips and caresses her body. there's soft jazz playing in the background, their movements slow and deliberate, lost in the moment.

Hours seem to pass in an instant as fall asleep still connected in an intimate embrace

Their connection has shifted, becoming something neither expected but both deeply feel.

The flight service staff loads an impressive array of shopping bags into the cargo hold as Mob-Lee and Destiny prepare to depart. Destiny laughs, watching the sheer number of items being packed.

"Do you think we went overboard?" she teases, leaning against the car.

"Nah," Mob-Lee replies with a smirk. "I told you—this trip was about you."

Once on the private jet and cruising at altitude, the conversation turns reflective. Destiny reclines in her seat, her expression soft. "You know, I've been thinking," she starts, turning to Mob-Lee. "I haven't spent a dime this whole trip—well, except for the scooter. And honestly, I've never had the luxury of not worrying about money until very recently. So tell me, Mr. Mitchell…" She leans forward, her eyes curious. "How much are you actually worth?"

Mob-Lee, caught mid-sip of water, chokes slightly. He sets his glass down, laughing. "Liquid or total assets?" he asks with a playful smirk.

Destiny narrows her eyes, caught off guard by his candor. "Do I even want to know?"

Without saying a word, Mob-Lee pulls out a sleek, blue metal bank card from his pocket and hands it to her. "There's two hundred on here."

"Two hundred million?" Destiny guesses, her tone filled with shock.

"No," Mob-Lee replies casually. "Two hundred billion. Liquid."

Destiny stares at him, her mouth slightly open.. The jet hums softly as five full minutes of silence pass. Finally, she cracks a smile and leans back in her seat. "Let me hold something real quick," she jokes, breaking the tension.

Both burst into laughter, their easy banter returning as they relax into the flight. As the conversation takes a more playful turn, they decide to test the limits of privacy aboard the jet.

At precisely 6:29 PM, the plane begins its descent into Jacksonville. As the wheels touch the tarmac, Destiny glances at her watch. It shifts to 6:30 on the dot.

Mob-Lee leans forward, calling to the cockpit. "Good job, Captain! She just checked her watch." He laughs as Destiny swats his arm, rolling her eyes but smiling.

As they disembark, Destiny turns to Mob-Lee, her expression thoughtful. "Would you join me for dinner at my mom's tonight? We usually get together every Sunday at 7:30."

"Sounds good," Mob-Lee replies, handing her phone back to her. "You left this in the seat pocket."

They power their phones back on for the first time in two days. Both devices light up with an avalanche of notifications. Destiny sees mostly work-related texts, with a few from her brother and mother. Mob-Lee's phone, however, floods with messages from Camille, Logan, Deuce, Vance, and several unknown numbers.

Mob-Lee signals to his driver to take his bags back to the estate. he and Destiny climb into her SUV, with Mob-Lee opting to let her take the lead.

As they navigate through Jacksonville's streets, Destiny opens up about her past. "I was adopted by Isabel Hunter when I was ten," she explains. "She's a remarkable woman. Some of the kids she fostered still come by for Sunday dinners. It's kind of a tradition."

Mob-Lee listens attentively. "She sounds like someone special."

"She is," Destiny says warmly. "And my brother —well, he's a bit of a jerk to guys I date, but he's harmless."

As they pull up to a stately home, Destiny's face lights up. "He's already here! You'll get to meet everyone I care about all at once."

Mob-Lee steps out of the SUV and helps the service staff unload a few the bags Destiny had gotten for her family. Inside, Destiny introduces him to Isabel Hunter, her foster mother. Isabel, a poised woman with a warm demeanor, greets Mob-Lee with genuine kindness.

"You must be Mob-Lee," Isabel says, extending her hand. "Destiny speaks very highly of you."

"The pleasure's mine, Ms. Hunter," Mob-Lee replies with a respectful nod.

While Destiny disappears down a hallway to check in with her brother, Mob-Lee assists the staff with the final bags.

As Mob-Lee stands in the entryway, he hears Destiny's laughter echoing from the hallway, accompanied by a deeper male voice.

"Oh, I can kill your new boyfriend if he ever has you gone like that with no phone again," the man jokes, his tone light but layered.

The footsteps grow louder until Destiny appears, arm in arm with her brother. "Kevin, this is Mob-Lee. Mob-Lee, this is my brother Kevin."

The two men lock eyes. Time seems to slow as realization dawns on both of them. Mob-Lee Mitchell and Kevin "TopBoy" Marks—sworn enemies —stand face-to-face for the first time.

They extend hands, maintaining a veneer of civility. The handshake is firm, almost testing, as unspoken tensions swirl beneath the surface.

"It's good to meet you," Kevin says, his voice steady but sharp.

"Likewise," Mob-Lee replies coolly.

Destiny, oblivious to the undercurrent, beams. "Great! Now let's eat."

The men exchange a brief glance, both understanding the fragile balance of the situation. The room feels charged, but for now, respect holds.

Chapter 13

The sun dips below the horizon, casting a golden hue over the beach. The night air carries a faint breeze as the sound of the ocean crashes gently against the shore. Diane Sterling's luxurious beachfront home stands serene against the encroaching dusk.

A slight knock echoes through the house. Edgar, Diane's trusted butler, answers the door with practiced professionalism. His face shifts slightly as he glances at the visitor, a tall, well-dressed man with an aura of authority. He steps aside without a word, allowing the stranger in.

In the back of the house, Diane and Stanley White meet in private, the tension between them palpable.

"Remember what we talked about," Stanley instructs in a low voice, his eyes scanning the room for any signs of danger. "Play it cool. Priority number one is keeping my name out of your mouth."

Diane nods, though her brow furrows slightly in confusion. Before she can voice any questions, a loud thud echoes from the front of the house. Both freeze, exchanging worried glances. The knock they heard earlier now feels wrong.

Suddenly, Diane's voice breaks the silence. "I'll check it out."

She moves toward the front of the house, her footsteps quickening with each passing second. She rounds the corner, and her breath catches in her throat. Edgar's body lies sprawled out on the floor, a pool of blood already spreading beneath him. Her scream shatters the air.

But before she can react further, the unmistakable sound of a pistol clicks from behind her. A chill runs down her spine as she turns slowly, her eyes locking onto a familiar face.

"Aura-Lee?" Diane breathes, her voice trembling.

Behind Aura-Lee, a looming shadow steps into view: Logan Livingston, his presence imposing. The cold steel of his weapon glints under the dim light.

Aura-Lee tilts her head, her short pixie cut reflecting the soft light of the room. "Sit down," she commands, her voice as sharp and controlled as ever. Diane, with no choice but to obey, sinks into the nearest chair, her heart pounding in her chest.

Stanley, hearing the commotion, bursts into the room. His face twists in anger as he sees the situation unfolding, but his charge at Aura-Lee is immediately thwarted. Logan steps forward, intercepting him with a swift motion. He delivers a punishing blow to the back of Stanley's head with the butt of his pistol, sending him sprawling to the floor in a daze.

"Sit down, both of you," Aura-Lee repeats, her voice unwavering.

Stanley groggily raises his head but remains silent, realizing the gravity of the situation. Diane, now paralyzed with fear, clenches her hands together, trying to remain calm.

Aura-Lee surveys them both, her gaze cold and calculating. "I know all about you, Diane. Or should I say... Dana Smith?"

Diane's face goes pale. "What are you talking about?"

Aura-Lee's lips curl into a knowing smile. "I did my homework. Your family came into money after your father won the lottery. He invested it in that nightclub. Your mom, with her MBA, made it profitable. Then, you changed your names and moved to the beach." She pauses, letting the weight of the revelation sink in. "I knew you looked familiar."

Diane's throat tightens as the past crashes over her like a wave. Aura-Lee's eyes flash with malicious satisfaction. "Remember back at Preeminence Preparatory Academy? That time you put Nair in that Black girl's special shampoo because she wouldn't share it with you?"

Aura-Lee pats her head, showcasing her own short, well-kept pixie cut. "You always did have a thing about hair, didn't you?"

The recognition is unmistakable. Diane's eyes widen in horror, the memory flooding back. She struggles to speak, but the words choke in her throat.

"Why?" Aura-Lee's voice is sharp, her gaze narrowing. "Why come after my family?"

Diane opens her mouth, but before she can speak, Aura-Lee raises a hand to silence her. "It doesn't matter. Just know this: The Mitchells remove all obstacles."

She turns to Stanley, her tone taking on a dark amusement. "And as for you, Mr. White... Grand Wizard White," she mocks. "You have three options."

Aura-Lee reaches into her pocket, pulling out a small snub-nose .38 revolver. She removes the bullets with methodical precision, leaving only one chambered. The weight of the gun in her hand feels oppressive.

"Option one," she continues, "you can use this bullet to kill her, and you become my personal dog. Option two, you can off yourself, and I'll release all your little secrets to the world. Option three," she looks up, her eyes darkening, "which I don't recommend, is to try to kill me. Logan will make sure you both die first."

Stanley's hand trembles slightly as he reaches for the gun, his mind racing with the weight of the decision. He stands frozen for a long moment, the choice bearing down on him.

Finally, he lifts the gun, his aim trained on Diane. She looks up at him, tears welling in her eyes, her voice a desperate plea. "Please... don't."

But Aura-Lee's voice cuts through the room like a blade. "You just made your choice, Stanley."

Stanley pulls the trigger sending pieces of Diane's brain flying against the wall.

Aura-Lee smiles coldly. "Now, thanks to your little side business and your ties to the Klan, I've got everything I need. Illegal dealings, your secrets, and now a murder." She leans forward, her voice a venomous whisper. "You'll hear from me soon. Don't try anything stupid."

She stands and gestures to Stanley. "Clean this up,"

Logan steps forward, his expression unreadable as he stares at Stanley. Aura-Lee turns and exits the room
her heels clicking sharply against the floor.

As she climbs into the sleek black G-Wagon
she pulls out her phone and taps out a quick message to Mob-Lee.

Need to talk.

A moment later, Mob-Lee's phone buzzes with a response

You'll never believe what I gotta tell you.

The tension is thick as the message sits unanswered. Aura-Lee leans back in the seat of the G-Wagon, her mind already racing through the next moves.

She glances out the window, the fading light of the evening casting long, distorted reflections on the glass. A dark feeling gnaws at her, knowing that the Mitchells power is growing and that the chessboard she's playing on is becoming more dangerous by the day.

As Logan drives, neither of them speak. The world outside passes by unnoticed, and all that remains is the ticking of time.

Mob-Lee stands on the front porch, the weight of Destiny Knight's revelation settling into his chest like a lead weight. Her brother? TopBoy? Of all people... His mind races as the pieces click together.

He pulls out his phone, thumb hesitating over Aura-Lee's contact. The message is simple but loaded.

You'll never believe what I gotta tell you.

The screen flickers as the message sends, and Mob-Lee exhales sharply, feeling like he's stepping into an even larger storm.

He starts the Bentley, the engine rumbling beneath him, but the soothing purr does little to calm his spinning mind. TopBoy. Destiny's foster brother. It was impossible.

The Mitchell Estate looms ahead, glowing under the estate's floodlights. Mob-Lee pulls into the driveway, only to see Aura-Lee's black G-Wagon trailing right behind him.

Aura-Lee steps out first, looking sharp but exhausted, her tailored jacket catching the faint breeze. Logan exits next, his imposing frame casting a long shadow as he scans their surroundings.

"Not even going to wait for us?" Aura-Lee teases as she approaches Mob-Lee's car.

"Didn't realize you were on my tail," Mob-Lee replies. "Big night?"

Aura-Lee sighs. "Bigger than it should've been. Diane Sterling turned out to be someone else entirely—Dana Smith, of all people. And Stanley White? Let's just say he's not running his mouth for a while."

Mob-Lee smirks. "Classic Aura-Lee cleanup. You get what you needed?"

"Enough," Aura-Lee replies, but there's a tension in her voice. "But let's hear your story. What's got you so distracted?"

Mob-Lee hesitates for a moment before dropping the bombshell. "TopBoy. is Destiny Knight's foster brother."

Aura-Lee freezes, her eyes narrowing. "What?"

"I found out tonight," Mob-Lee says, his voice low.

Aura-Lee's expression shifts from disbelief to cold calculation. "You're serious."

"As a heart attack," Mob-Lee confirms.

Aura-Lee closes her eyes, taking a steadying breath. "Library. One hour. I need a minute to clean up and clear my head." She strides toward the house without another word.

Logan hangs back as Aura-Lee disappears into the house, his stoic expression unreadable.

"You're backing her story?" Mob-Lee asks, leaning against the Bentley.

Logan nods. "Every detail. Diane Sterling—Dana Smith—got what she deserved. And Stanley White won't be causing any issues, at least for now."

Mob-Lee raises an eyebrow. "At least for now?"

Logan's jaw tightens. "Because there's something bigger at play."

"What's going on?"

Logan steps closer, lowering his voice. "Boys from the Bottom hit several coastline spots tonight. Heavy casualties. Loss of product."

Mob-Lee's stomach sinks. "How bad?"

"Bad enough to turn the families into a hornet's nest. They're already calling for blood."

Mob-Lee exhales, his mind racing. "What's needed from me?"

Logan's expression softens slightly. "Nothing yet. Let us assess the damage first. I'll let you know."

Logan places a firm hand on Mob-Lee's shoulder before heading inside, leaving Mob-Lee to grapple with the gravity of the situation.

Mob-Lee barely makes it past the grand staircase when Vance Cruz steps into his path, his usual swagger replaced with unease.

"Got a minute?" Vance asks, his voice lower than usual.

Mob-Lee's eyes narrow. "Depends."

"This isn't a joke," Vance snaps. "It's about Bernard Dubois."

Mob-Lee folds his arms. "What about him?"

"He's still looking for payment," Vance says, his voice tight. "And if he doesn't get it soon, he's going to make an example out of someone."

Mob-Lee's expression hardens. "And what does that have to do with me?"

Vance hesitates, clearly reluctant to answer. "Dubois thinks you're a threat to the his business. He's circling because he knows we're vulnerable."

"Sounds like a you problem, not a me problem," Mob-Lee retorts.

Vance steps closer, his voice dropping to a hiss. "It'll be everyone's problem if he escalates. Fix it, or he'll burn us all."

Mob-Lee stares him down. "Then you'd better make sure he doesn't get the chance."

Vance's jaw tightens, but he steps aside, letting Mob-Lee continue toward his quarters.

Mob-Lee opens the door to his quarters, expecting solitude. Instead, he finds Aunt Camille sitting on one of his chairs, her hands clasped tightly together.

"Aunt Cammy?" he says, surprised.

"I needed to talk to you," she says quietly, her tone uncharacteristically vulnerable.

Mob-Lee sits across from her, his curiosity piqued. "What's this about?"

Camille hesitates, then speaks. "I know you have the family files. And I know you've been reading them."

Mob-Lee leans back, arms crossed. "And?"

"I need you to understand something," she begins, her voice trembling slightly. "The day of the gala, I received a threat. Someone knows about a decision I made years ago. A bribe."

Mob-Lee raises an eyebrow. "Go on."

"A large corporation wanted me to uphold a law that allowed them to steal and sell private data. Millions of Americans lost their privacy freedoms—and in many cases, their income—because of that decision. And I upheld it... for money," she confesses, her voice breaking.

Mob-Lee's expression darkens. "are you still receiving money from it?"

Camille nods. "Yes. And now, someone is threatening to expose everything. If they do, it'll ruin me—and the family."

Mob-Lee exhales, the weight of her words sinking in. "Do you know who's behind the threat?"

She shakes her head. "Not yet. But we need to find out. Fast."

Alone at last, Mob-Lee stares out the window, his mind racing. Destiny's connection to TopBoy. The Mafia attacks. Vance's warning about Bernard Dubois. Aunt Camille's confession. It all feels like an avalanche, threatening to bury him.

He opens his laptop, the glow illuminating his face as he pulls up the family files. The secrets they hold could destroy the Mitchell legacy—or save it.

Time to start connecting the dots, he thinks grimly, his fingers flying across the keyboard.

The night stretches on as Mob-Lee begins to plan his next move, knowing there's no turning back.

Rain streaks the windshield as Kevin Marks Jr., aka TopBoy, weaves through traffic, his jaw clenched. His car's Bluetooth connects, and he dials BabyBoy. The line picks up after a single ring.

"Yo," BabyBoy answers, his voice low and hurried.

"What's the update?" Kevin demands, his tone clipped, his fingers gripping the steering wheel.

BabyBoy exhales heavily, static crackling over the line. "Kev, it's bad. Feds showed up at the spot with a warrant. They ain't playin' this time. Shit's way too hot right now."

Kevin's stomach tightens. "What else?"

BabyBoy hesitates, his pause loaded with tension. "The Y.Ns..." He trails off, then adds, "...they did it big."

Kevin's foot eases off the accelerator as dread washes over him. "What does 'big' mean, bruh?" His voice sharpens, each word razor-edged.

"Word is, they hit a neutral zone, Kev," BabyBoy finally spits out. "Not just Coastline Mafia. Civilians. Cops. Shit went sideways in the worst way."

Kevin's hand slams the dashboard, the sound echoing in the small cabin. "Tell me you're joking."

"I wish I was," BabyBoy replies, his voice heavy with unease. "People are talkin'. It's bad out here."

Kevin's mind races as he pulls onto a quieter street, his breathing shallow. "I'm heading down there. so keep your eyes open. I need to see this for myself."

"Top, I'm serious—it's hot as hell in the Bottom. Be smart, man," BabyBoy warns.

Kevin doesn't reply, ending the call abruptly. He grips the wheel, his knuckles white, as he steers toward the Bottom.

Kevin approaches the infamous Car Wash Corner, his car slowing as the flashing lights of emergency vehicles flood the street.

The neighborhood is alive with chaos. Red, white, and blue lights spin in a dizzying dance, reflecting off wet pavement. A perimeter of police tape blocks the main road, and Kevin watches as officers bark orders at a crowd of onlookers. Paramedics wheel gurneys to waiting ambulances, the white sheets covering bodies stained with crimson.

Kevin's chest tightens as he surveys the scene, his gut twisting at the gravity of the situation. Then, a sleek black SUV catches his eye, parked just beyond the police barricade.

Inside, he sees Logan "Dutchie" Livingston behind the wheel, Deuce in the passenger seat, and—his breath catches—Mob-Lee Mitchell sitting in the back, driver's side window.

Kevin's mind ignites, memories and emotions colliding in a storm of fury.

He was at my mom's house.
He's dating my sister.
He's a member of Coastline Mafia.
He killed my guys.
I've got a score to settle.

Kevin's teeth grind, his rage simmering just below the surface. His hand hovers over his phone, tempted to make a move, but instead, he slams the gas and peels away.

He pulls into a side street, the rain pounding against the car as he dials a number.

A sultry voice answers after the first ring. "Hey, stranger," she says, her tone dripping with warmth.

"Hey," Kevin replies, his voice calmer than he feels. "It's too hot in the Bottom tonight. Mind if I crash at your place?"

"You know you're always welcome," she says with a soft laugh. "You okay, though? You sound... off."

"I'm good," he lies. "Just need to lay low for a bit."

"I'll leave the door unlocked," she promises.

Kevin ends the call and leans back in his seat, staring out at the rain-soaked street. The weight of the night presses heavily on his shoulders.

Kevin sits on a plush couch, a glass of whiskey in his hand. He stares blankly at the television as his phone vibrates on the table.

He picks it up, frowning at the unknown number. "What the hell?" he mutters before answering.

A cold, robotic voice greets him. "You have a call from the Federal Bureau of Prisons. Do you accept the call?"

Kevin hesitates, his gut twisting. "Yeah. I accept."

There's a brief pause, then a voice begins reciting a string of numbers:

"9 1 2 5 5 5 2 2 2 2. Call it."

They repeat the numbers three times before the line goes dead.

Kevin stares at the phone, the numbers burned into his memory. He sets the whiskey glass down and dials.

The call connects, and Kevin hears the familiar, enraged voice of his father, BigBoy, on the other end.

"What the fuck did you do?!" BigBoy's voice booms, filled with unrelenting fury.

Kevin's heart pounds in his chest. "What are you talking about?"

"Don't play dumb with me!" BigBoy snarls. "You sent your little idiots into the only goddamn spot that's off-limits and let them massacre everyone?!"

Kevin sits up straighter, his voice rising in confusion. "I didn't send anyone! What spot?"

"The neutral zone, Junior! A fucking neutral zone! You know what that means? Civilians, cops, allies—everyone! They slaughtered them all! You think that's just gonna blow over?!"

Kevin's stomach churns as the realization hits him. "I didn't give that order," he says, his voice shaking.

"Then you've lost control of your people," BigBoy spits venomously. "And now, we're all screwed because of it! Feds are breathing down our necks, Coastline Mafia wants blood, and every other crew in the city is watching us burn. Fix this, Junior. You've got 24 hours, or I swear to God, you'll wish you were one of the bodies in that neutral zone!"

The line goes dead.

Kevin lowers the phone slowly, his hand trembling. His chest heaves as he tries to steady his breathing. The weight of the situation crashes down on him, suffocating.

"24 hours," he whispers to himself. His eyes darken as he grabs his jacket and heads for the door. There's no time to waste.

He wasn't going to fix it out of loyalty to his father.
He was going to fix it because his survival—and his pride—depended on it.

Tah-Mary's Lounge, the next Morning. The rising sun does little to soften the grisly scene. Yellow police tape flutters in the breeze, surrounding the gutted remains of the once-bustling neutral zone. Broken glass crunches underfoot as Detective Aiden Finn steps out of his car, his eyes narrowing at the carnage before him. Officer Mike Furman stands nearby, his face pale as he talks to a uniformed officer.

Finn approaches, his hands shoved into his coat pockets. He and Furman exchange a grim look, their expressions betraying a mutual understanding.

"Last time we met, it was BFTB bodies on the ground," Finn says, his voice low. "Now it's Coastline's turn."

Furman nods, swallowing hard. "And everyone else in between. Civilians, cops… hell, there's even a councilman in there." He points toward the shattered front window of Tah-Mary's, where a pair of legs in a sharp suit stick out from beneath a bloodstained table.

Finn lets out a slow breath, stepping closer to the entrance. The smell of death hits him immediately—a pungent mix of copper, charred wood, and spilled alcohol. Inside, bodies are slumped over tables and sprawled across the floor. Blood stains every surface, pooling beneath shattered bottles and overturned chairs.

"This wasn't just an attack," Finn mutters. "This was a message."

Furman steps in behind him, careful not to disturb the evidence. "Tah-Mary's was Switzerland. Cops, dealers, politicians… everyone knew this was neutral ground. Whoever did this didn't just break the rules—they burned the whole damn rulebook."

Finn crouches beside a body wearing a Coastline jacket, the insignia smeared with blood. "And TopBoy's never been this reckless before," he says. "Not like this."

Furman shakes his head. "Reckless or not, this is his work. BFTB hit them here, and now Coastline's going to go scorched earth in the Bottom."

Finn stands, his gaze sweeping over the room. "Neutral or not, this was still Coastline territory. Someone had the balls to come here and massacre everyone. Whoever ordered this knew exactly what they were doing."

Finn and Furman barely have time to process the scene at Tah-Mary's when Furman's radio crackles to life.

"Units, we've got a confirmed drive-by on Smyrna. Multiple fatalities. Possible gang affiliation—BFTB."

Finn and Furman exchange a look. "That didn't take long," Finn mutters, already heading for the door.

Smyrna Drive, Later. The scene is chaotic. Seven bodies lie in the street, riddled with bullets, surrounded by shattered glass and smoking wreckage. Residents watch from behind closed doors and drawn curtains, their fear palpable.

Finn steps out of the car, scanning the scene. "BFTB," he says, pointing to the distinctive tattoos on the victims' arms. "Coastline's answer to Tah-Mary's."

Furman steps over to one of the bodies, shaking his head. "They didn't just hit them—they butchered them. Look at this." He gestures to the body of a young man whose face is barely recognizable. "This wasn't just about killing. This was personal."

Finn's jaw tightens. "Retaliation always is. Tah-Mary's wasn't just a hit—it was a declaration of war. Coastline's making sure everyone knows what happens when you cross them."

Back in the car, Finn and Furman sit in silence for a moment, the weight of the day settling over them.

"We can't let this spiral out of control," Furman says finally. "If we don't figure out who ordered the Tah-Mary's hit, it's only going to get worse."

Finn rubs his temples, his eyes focused on the road ahead. "It's already worse. Tah-Mary's wasn't just a Coastline spot—it was neutral ground for everyone in the city. Killing everyone in there was like throwing a grenade into a hornet's nest."

Furman sighs, leaning back in his seat. "So what's the play? We can't just knock on TopBoy's door and ask him to call a truce."

Finn shakes his head. "No, but we can start with the people who had the most to gain from hitting Tah-Mary's. Someone wanted this war, and they made damn sure it started. We just have to figure out who."

Furman frowns, his mind racing. "You think this came from inside BFTB?"

Finn's eyes narrow. "It had to. No one else would risk hitting Coastline's neutral zone unless they had something to prove. And whoever did it wanted to make sure there were no witnesses."

Later that evening, Finn and Furman sit in the precinct, going over files and surveillance footage. The tension between them is thick as they try to piece together the puzzle.

"Look at this," Finn says, pointing to a grainy image from a traffic camera near Tah-Mary's. "Black SUV, no plates. That's our shooter."

Furman leans over, studying the image. "Doesn't exactly narrow it down. Half of BFTB rolls around in SUVs."

Finn flips through another file, his jaw tightening. "Then we start with their inner circle. TopBoy's not stupid—he wouldn't greenlight something like this unless he had a damn good reason. We find out who made the call, we stop this war before it gets worse."

Furman raises an eyebrow. "You think this is just the beginning?"

Finn's expression hardens. "I know it is. BFTB just poked the biggest bear in the city. And now we're all going to pay for it."

Finn's Apartment, Finn sits at his desk, surrounded by files and notes. His phone buzzes, the caller ID blocked. He answers hesitantly.

"Detective Finn."

A distorted voice responds. "You're playing a dangerous game, Detective."

Finn's grip tightens on the phone. "Who is this?"

The voice chuckles darkly. "Someone who knows how this ends. Stay out of the way, or you'll end up like the rest of them."

Finn's jaw clenches. "People are dying because of this war. You think I'm just going to stand by and watch?"

The voice lowers. "You won't have a choice if you're dead."

The line goes dead, leaving Finn staring at the phone, his determination hardening. He knows he's up against forces far larger than himself—but he's not about to back down.

Back on the Miami Strip, Neon lights pulse against the humid air as Brandon Corvin strolls down the bustling street with a group of well-dressed associates. The crowd moves with the rhythm of the nightlife, the scent of ocean salt mixing with cologne and alcohol.

Brandon's phone buzzes in his pocket. He glances at the screen, frowning as he sees the name flash across.

Brandon (answering): "Corvin."

There's a pause before a familiar voice responds, trembling slightly.

Tasha: "Brandon… It's me."

Brandon (flatly): "Tasha."

Tasha: "They let me out on bond… I've been in federal custody for two weeks. What are we going to do?"

Brandon slows his pace, his associates walking ahead without noticing his distraction. His expression hardens, and his tone becomes icy.

Brandon: "'We'? Bitch, did you learn French in jail?"

Tasha is silent on the other end, the sharpness of his words cutting through her resolve.

Brandon (coldly): "Here's what we're going to do. You're not going to call me. Ever again."

He hangs up without waiting for her response, slipping his phone back into his pocket and rejoining his group. But the carefree energy of the night has faded. His mind races, calculating his next move.

Tasha sits on the edge of her couch, her hands trembling as she clutches her phone. The dim light of a single lamp casts long shadows on the walls. Her face is streaked with tears, her breath hitching as she alternates between anger, regret, and despair.

Tasha scrolls through her contacts, her thumb hovering over Mob-Lee's name. Her mind flashes with images of his face, the weight of her betrayal pressing down on her chest.

Tasha (to herself): "I should call him… I should explain."

Her finger moves to Brandon's number, but his harsh words replay in her mind, stopping her. She lets out a frustrated sob, tossing the phone onto the cushion beside her.

Tasha (whispering): "Or I could call the feds. Burn it all down."

She buries her face in her hands, torn between self-preservation and revenge.

Mob-Lee sits in his car in the sprawling driveway, the vast estate looming behind him. His phone is pressed to his ear as he speaks to Deuce, his voice steady and determined.

Mob-Lee: "Yeah, I'm in. Whatever Coastline needs, I'm there. Just let me know the plan."

He ends the call and exhales deeply, resting his head against the seat. The weight of the war and his commitment to Coastline settle over him. His phone buzzes again, and he answers without checking the ID.

Mob-Lee: "Talk."

There's a pause, followed by a deep, gravelly voice that instantly commands his attention.

Voice: "Son. Watch everybody."

Mob-Lee freezes, his grip tightening on the phone.

Mob-Lee: "Dad?"

The line goes dead, leaving Mob-Lee staring at the screen, his heart pounding. He looks out into the darkness of the estate, his instincts screaming that something is about to happen.

Brandon Corvin sits alone in a sleek, modern apartment overlooking the city. A glass of bourbon rests untouched on the table as he paces, his mind racing.

He grabs his phone and begins typing notes, creating contingency plans to protect himself from any potential fallout with Tasha.

Brandon (to himself): "If she even thinks about talking to the feds, I'll have to shut her down. For good."

He stops pacing, looking out over the city with a cold, calculating expression.

Brandon: "She's a loose end now. And loose ends get cut."

Later That Night. Mob-Lee stands outside his car, staring into the darkness. His father's voice echoes in his mind.

Mob-Lee: "Watch everybody."

He looks around, the quiet of the estate suddenly feeling oppressive. His phone buzzes again, this time a text from Deuce.

Deuce (text): "Change of plans. Meet me at the docks. Midnight."

Mob-Lee pockets his phone, his instincts telling him that whatever is coming will change everything. He steps back into his car, the engine roaring to life as he drives off into the night.

Made in the USA
Columbia, SC
08 February 2025